The Moniker

Sweetwater Close #2

A Rumpelstiltskin story

By Cyan Tayse

Published by Stacey Broadbent, Ashburton, NZ
Copyright 2022 © Cyan Tayse

Proofreading by Spell Bound
Cover image from Deposit Photos
Cover Design by Stacey Broadbent

ISBN: 978-0-473-64989-9 (paperback)
        978-0-473-64987-6 (kindle)

The Moniker

Sweetwater Close #2

A Rumpelstiltskin story

By Cyan Tayse

Contents

Author's Note

The characters in this story are from a fictitious setting, and as I am from New Zealand, UK spelling and terms have been used. Please remember these are not errors, it's just the way we do things here.

Chapter 1

The Ex

"We had a deal, Melissa." Joe scowled at her small frame as she stood with her hands folded across her chest. "It's my weekend to have her."

"She's not some business deal you can broker, *Joe*. She's our daughter. And if she doesn't want to go with you, I'm not going to make her."

"You're far too lenient on her. She needs to learn to follow rules."

Melissa scoffed. "*Your* rules, you mean?" She shook her head. "Vaughn follows—"

"Her name is Siobhan, not Vaughn," he interrupted.

"I'm well aware of her name, but she prefers to go by Vaughn. I've explained this to you before."

"Vaughn is a boy's name. Not that you can tell she's a girl by the way you allow her to dress."

"Excuse me?"

"You heard me. Her hair is cut short, and it's always a different colour every time I see her. She wears baggy hoodies with jeans and those ungodly chunky boots most days. It's hardly very feminine."

Melissa fought back the urge to slap him. *He's the father of your child*, she reminded herself as she took a calming breath.

"Vaughn can dress however she wants to. It doesn't make her any less your daughter if she wants to go by a different name and wear clothes you don't approve of. In fact, it's kind of in the textbook of being a teenager. Don't you remember being her age?" He stared blankly at her. "Oh, that's right. You were born in a tailored suit with a briefcase in your hand, weren't you?" She rolled her eyes. It was moments like this that made her question how she even managed to procreate with a man like Joe Balderson.

"Of course you'd take the childish route, wouldn't you?" Joe stretched his arm out, letting the sleeve of his shirt ride up, revealing his gold Hugo Boss watch. "I don't have time for this. Siobhan!" he called out.

"Joe, stop. I told you, she's not coming with you this weekend." She lowered her voice, stepping closer. "Listen, she's going through some things at the moment, and she just wants to be home with me right now. Okay? You can have her next weekend instead. Two weeks in a row."

"That's not the deal we had, and you know it. I can take you to court for this, Melissa. I have every right to see her. Need I remind you of the contract you signed?"

"I'm well aware of the bloody contract," she hissed. When he'd packed his bags and walked out the door, Joe had gone straight to the lawyers. Not because he was the doting father, but to prove he had the power to take her. She still had no idea why he'd given in in the end. "But surely you can allow her to have this one weekend at home?"

"She'll be perfectly fine at *my* home."

Melissa huffed out an agitated breath. "You're being unreasonable."

"I'm doing no such thing." He stepped around her. "Siobhan!"

"It's okay, Mum." Vaughn shuffled through the door. "I can go."

"Oh, honey." She shot Joe a warning look before rushing over to her daughter. "I'm sorry you had to hear all that," she said quietly, brushing a gelled strand of hair from Vaughn's forehead and watching it flick straight back to the same place. Her palms settled on her daughter's arms. "You don't have to go if you don't want to. I can deal with him."

"I know." Vaughn glanced at her father before nodding. "I'll be okay."

Melissa pulled her into her arms. "Are you sure?" she whispered.

"Mmhmm."

"Have you got…" Melissa glanced towards Vaughn's stomach before continuing, "Everything you need?"

"Yeah. I took some Naprogesic before, and I'll put the packet in my bag along with… everything else."

Melissa smoothed her hands down Vaughn's hair, pulling her face in until their foreheads touched. "I'm sorry, baby. I tried," she whispered, hating that Joe would rather wave his dick around than pay attention to his daughter's feelings. Being a fifteen-year-old wasn't

11

easy at the best of times, and having puberty rear its ugly head on his weekend, of all times, was the icing on the cake.

As soon as Vaughn had begun complaining of a sore back, she'd known. She'd been a late bloomer herself, and she remembered all too well the signs of that first time.

"I don't have all day, Melissa." Joe tapped his polished shoe against the floor, and every tap felt like a blade through her back.

"Text me if you need anything, okay?" She reached down and grabbed the small bag Vaughn had brought out with her. "Anything at all."

"Thanks, Mum."

"Oh for goodness sake. It's two nights, Melissa. Cut the cords already." He snatched the bag from her hand, turning toward the door. "If she needs anything, I'm perfectly capable of providing it for her."

Melissa gritted her teeth to stop from snapping at him, instead holding her phone up and giving Vaughn a pointed look.

With a defeated smile, Vaughn trailed after her father. She climbed into his pompous black Mercedes with blacked-out windows, and then she was gone.

Chapter 2

The friend

"I bring wine and chips." Jane bustled through the door waving a bottle of red through the air. "I hope you like merlot."

"I'll take anything right now." Melissa took the wine from her hand and made her way through to the kitchen. Pulling two wine glasses down from the cabinet, she opened the bottle and poured the glasses to the brim.

Jane eyed her with a raised brow. "That bad, huh?" She pulled a chair out from the breakfast bar and sat down. "What happened?"

Melissa held her finger in the air as she tipped her glass back, taking a hefty gulp. She let out a sigh as she placed it back on the counter. "Joe Balderson, that's what happened." She shook her head. "He can be such a pretentious arse sometimes." She ripped the bag of chips open and tipped them into a bowl, taking one before sliding it into the centre of the bar.

"Sometimes?" Jane smirked, and Melissa chuckled. It wasn't the first time they'd had this conversation.

"You're right. He's always an arse, but this time it was towards Vaughn." She frowned into her glass. "He doesn't understand what it's like being a teenage girl, and he's not even willing to try to understand either." She took another gulp of her wine. "He insists on calling her Siobhan too, which really irks me. She's asked him time and time again to call her Vaughn, but he won't budge."

Jane rolled her eyes. "Of course he won't. Remind me again how you ended up doing the nasty with him? Because the two of you together do not make sense."

"Believe me, I've asked myself that same question many times." She dragged the bowl of chips back towards her and grabbed a handful while eyeing her phone.

"Just text her. It'll put your mind at ease."

"I know it would, but does it seem too overbearing? He told me to cut the cords." She grimaced. "Am I that bad?"

Jane placed her glass on the counter and pushed up from her seat. She walked around the counter and lay her hands on Melissa's shoulders. "You're her mum. It's your job to worry and sometimes be overbearing." She nodded at the phone then nudged it toward her. "Go on. I know you won't relax until you know she's okay."

Melissa pulled her lips into a thin line, then quickly snatched the phone up. She stabbed at the screen a few times then huffed out a breath and set the phone back down.

"Feel better?"

"I will once she answers me."

With two fingers, Jane raised Melissa's chin. "A watched phone never pings." A high-pitched trill rang out and the phone vibrated against the counter. "See? I told you." She winked, scooping the phone up and handing it to her.

Melissa's eyes darted back and forth as she scanned the message, then her shoulders sagged and she let out a sigh. "She's fine. Her cramps have eased, and they're just heading out to dinner."

"Speaking of dinner…" Jane quirked her brow. "Have you eaten anything other than chips?"

The look on Melissa's face made it obvious she hadn't. The printer had malfunctioned at work, and it was a mad dash to get the gazette out on time. She'd survived on coffee and adrenaline all day.

"How about I take *you* out for dinner then?" Jane grabbed the wine glass from Melissa's hand before she could take another mouthful. "Red wine on an empty stomach is a recipe for disaster. It's like drinking etiquette 101. Believe me, you do *not* want to be up at two in the morning, throwing that back up again. Red on the way in, red on the way out." She shuddered. "That's a sight I won't forget. I thought I was dying."

Melissa scrunched her nose. She'd never been much of a drinker, just the occasional one to calm her nerves in social situations or when dealing with her ex. Suffice to say, she'd been imbibing a little more of late.

"That doesn't sound appealing at all." She grabbed another handful of chips, popping one in her mouth and crunching. "I suppose dinner would be a good idea."

"Good. I'll make us a reservation."

Melissa glanced down at her jeans and tee then over to the crisp pantsuit Jane was sporting. "Guess I should go change."

Jane shrugged. "You look fine as you are."

Snorting, Melissa brushed past Jane and through to the hall. "Places that take reservations have dress codes, and somehow I doubt ripped jeans fit the bill."

"I don't know. Lucious is always dressed casual when we go in there."

"And Lucious is the mayor's son. He's one of the founding families. He can do whatever he wants. *I*, on the other hand, am a lowly journalist for the free paper." She cupped her hands in front of her, as if comparing the weight of fruit. "Totally different."

Jane's brow furrowed. "Don't do that. There's nothing wrong with doing what you love. And you're hardly *just* a journalist. You own the damn thing. Believe me, there is nothing lowly about you, Melissa Hobart. Nothing at all."

Melissa smiled and nodded, unconvinced. "I'll just be a sec." She padded down the hall to her room, unbuttoning her jeans as she went. It had been a while since anyone other than Vaughn had bothered enough to check in on her, and make sure she was looking after herself. She had a tendency to overlook her own needs on a regular basis. And after going head-to-head with Joe, Jane was like a breath of fresh air. She wasn't trying to prove anything or one-up her, and she certainly didn't try to push her buttons like Joe did.

Their relationship had been one of timing and convenience more than anything. He had been a friend of her father's, and though he was some years older than her, they had been pushed together. She, fresh from college and eager to make a name for herself in the world of journalism, had jumped at the opportunities afforded to her when she was on his arm.

The Balderson name was synonymous with Gold in the corporate world. Literally. He was one of the most well-known and sought-after bankers and investors in the country. He'd promised her the world, and for a time, she'd had it. His name was all she'd needed to secure herself a job working for one of the largest news agents in the area. And things had been glorious until Melissa had become pregnant and decided to take a step back. It was enough to sour their relationship.

Joe didn't want his name belonging to someone with no ambition; which was how he saw her. Not as the mother of his child, but as someone who had given up her dreams and aspirations to play house. It didn't help that he hadn't been particularly pleased with the pregnancy in the first place, claiming to be too old to be a father.

They'd survived two years after Vaughn was born before he finally walked out.

She'd packed up what little she had and moved them to Sweetwater Close where she put her skills to use on her own enterprise. The Sweetwater Gazette. It was a free paper distributed around the area, and it was her second pride and joy, after Vaughn. She was no longer a name to be recognised or sought after, but Jane was right; she was doing what she loved, and not many could say the same thing.

Even so, she wasn't going to be caught wearing ripped jeans to a swanky restaurant. She rummaged through her wardrobe until she found a long black skirt with a slit up the side and paired it with a baby blue chiffon shirt that cinched at the waist. She slipped a pair of ballet flats on her feet and joined Jane back in the kitchen.

"Wow." Jane's eyes seemed to drink her in as they trailed up and down her length. "You look great."

Melissa's cheeks flushed as she gave a twirl, her hands held palm up. "Why thank you."

"You ready to go?" Jane held her hand out, and Melissa took it with a smile. A flush of heat filled her stomach and warmed her chest as Jane entwined their fingers, swinging their hands gently between them.

"Yes." It came out breathy, and she knew she was blushing again. Jane brought out feelings she'd long since laid to rest. After what she went through with Joe, she hadn't been willing to enter another relationship, but the more time she spent with Jane, the more she thought it might be a possibility. Everything felt easy around her. Natural.

But aside from holding hands, nothing more had happened between them, and she sometimes wondered if it would. When Joe walked out and took his connections with him, it had been a blow to her ego. The people she'd thought were her colleagues and friends were all in his pockets, and they'd dumped her before the ink on the divorce papers was dry. She'd been left with nothing and no one except Vaughn.

She didn't trust easily anymore, and giving her heart to someone new terrified her, but at the same time, it filled her with something she hadn't felt in a long time. Hope.

Chapter 3

The dinner date

The restaurant was on the corner across from Giancarlos. It had the kind of dim lighting that was meant to create ambience, but really just made it difficult to read a menu. Large pillars broke up the room, and a deep burgundy carpet lined the floors. The walls had a stippled look to them, with bursts of gold amongst the pale peach paint, and fairy lights ran across the edgings and hung low in each corner.

It had become one of Jane's favourite haunts after spending so much time lunching there while Lucious was still pining over Raoul, before they finally took the plunge and got together. It had taken them long enough.

"Can I get you ladies anything to drink?" the waiter asked as he showed them to their seats.

"A bottle of merlot, please. And water for the table." Jane draped her jacket over the back of her seat before sitting down.

The waiter nodded, bouncing on the heels of his feet. "Of course." He wove through the tables to the bar, leaving them to themselves.

"Thank you for this," Melissa said. "I needed to get out of the house before I drove myself insane with worry."

Jane waved a dismissive hand. "This is just as much for me as it is for you." She leaned across the table, lowering her voice. "I get hangry if I don't eat."

"You and me both." Melissa laughed. She knew the feeling all too well. Back when she'd been younger, she could go a whole day without a meal, forgetting her appetite until the evening when she became ravenous. Since becoming a mother, she found her hunger had become more insistent and wreaked havoc on her emotions, but it didn't stop her from neglecting her appetite at times of stress. Thankfully, she hadn't passed that trait onto Vaughn.

Opening the menu, Melissa scanned the options. "It all sounds delicious. What do you recommend?"

"The salmon is to die for. Melts in your mouth." She held her fingers to her lips in a chef's kiss. "Magnifique."

"Alright, I'll give that a go then." She closed the menu and pushed it aside.

Jane quirked a brow. "You're easy to please."

Melissa shrugged. "It takes me an age to choose, and I trust your judgement. No point deliberating when I've got a perfect recommendation right there in front of me."

"You do make an excellent point, and clearly I have good taste. Look at the company I keep."

Melissa's cheeks flamed once more, and she was beginning to wish she hadn't opted for the jacket she was still wearing. As she went to push her sleeves up, a raucous laugh burst from a bespectacled woman at the bar who was being overly flirtatious with the man beside her. Melissa watched as she threw her head back, her two chins wobbling as she laughed. The fingers of her right hand curled around the forearm of the man who'd captured her attention, and a lascivious smile spread across his face.

Oh to be so open about your feelings, however lust-filled they were. It made her feel even more awkward.

"Speaking of company," Jane continued, pulling her attention back, "I was at the youth centre the other day with Lucious. Vaughn's art wall is really starting to take shape."

When Raoul had taken over running the Sweetwater Youth, one of the first things he did was ask Vaughn to paint a mural on one of the bare walls. Melissa hadn't seen Vaughn so focused and excited about a project in a long time.

"Yeah? I wish I could see it, but she won't let me until it's finished."

"Oh, it's quite something. She has a real talent. If she's looking at going to art school, this would most definitely tip the scales in her favour."

Pride blossomed in Melissa's chest. She couldn't draw to save herself, but Vaughn had had a knack for it since the first moment she was able to hold a crayon in her chubby little fingers. In fact, there were two large plastic containers in the hall cupboard filled to the brim with every painting and drawing she'd brought home from preschool and school. The fridge had always been covered in her creations, and the hall was a sort of shrine to her work, holding Melissa's favoured pieces in frames.

Art school is all Vaughn has talked about for the past few years, and Melissa would do anything in her power to help her get there. Knowing there were others willing to back her, meant the world to her. Especially when Joe was adamant she'd be studying business or banking and following in his footsteps. He saw her art as a hobby, not a means to earn a living.

"Do you think Raoul or Lucious would write her a recommendation? I know it would mean a lot to her if they did. She thinks the world of them both."

"Are you kidding? Raoul has a crazy soft spot for her. He'll definitely write one, and Lucious will too, if he knows what's good for him."

Melissa laughed. "You have that much control over what he does?"

"I like to think of it as more of a mutual respect." She stuck her tongue between her teeth. "I know too much about him for him to turn me down. And anyway, he can see the talent she has, and he's all about following your heart."

"You make him sound like the perfect guy."

"Mmm, he's far from perfect, but he's definitely one of the good ones. I lucked out when I got assigned to be his PA. For all the crap I give him, it's actually a pretty cruisy job. I basically get paid to hang out and give him shit."

"Living the dream." Melissa chuckled. "I wish someone would pay me to just hang out. Believe it or not, there's not a lot of money to be made in a free newspaper." She picked at the corner of her napkin, folding it over.

Jane gasped in mock horror. "You mean you're not a multi-millionaire?"

"Shocking, right? I know I appear to be well off with my ripped mum jeans and faded band tees, but alas, it is not the case." She fluttered her eyelashes, holding a hand to her chest.

The waiter appeared by the table, clearing his throat. "Your drink." He held his arm out, draped in a white towel, and held the bottle against it.

"That'll do nicely." Jane nodded, and the waiter unscrewed the bottle, pouring them both a glass then placing it on the table between them. He took their orders and assured them a pitcher of water would be arriving at the table momentarily, then he turned on his heels and disappeared through the crowd.

Melissa raised her glass to her lips, taking a sip. She let out a sigh. "This is nice. I don't go out enough."

"Well, I am always up for a girls' night." Jane leaned back in her seat. "Or if you just need to vent about exes—" she pointed two thumbs at her chest, "—I'm your gal."

"Thanks. I just might take you up on that. I'm sure you're not surprised to hear that Joe gets on my wick on a regular basis." She took another swig of her wine before remembering Jane's warning. Pushing the glass farther away, she turned her attention to the cutlery, lining each up against the other.

"It doesn't surprise me in the least." Jane reached a hand across, placing it atop Melissa's to stop her fidgeting. "All jokes aside, I'm here whenever you need someone to talk to or take your mind off things, okay? My life revolves around Luscious most of the time, and it's nice to have someone else to occupy my time. So, really, *you'd* be doing *me* a favour."

"Says the woman being paid to hang out and have fun." She grinned, wrapping her thumb around Jane's. "But I get it. My life pretty much revolves around Vaughn and The Sweetwater Gazette."

"Well, now you have me to add to the list." Jane smiled, her eyes falling to their joined hands. She slid hers around, palm up, to slip beneath Melissa's. Their fingers curling into each other's.

Melissa swallowed thickly, her cheeks heating. She cleared her throat to speak but was interrupted by the waiter placing a carafe of water on the table. They pulled apart.

"Are we ready to order, ladies?"

Chapter 4

The next day

Thoughts of Jane and the way she'd held her hand the night before kept playing on Melissa's mind. Even walking in the brisk morning air with an audiobook playing through her headphones wasn't enough to distract her from Jane and her alluring hands.

Part of her wanted to see where it might lead, while the other more practical part of her was scared to ruin the friendship that had blossomed over the past few months. When Vaughn had introduced them after the mid-year show, there had been a stirring inside Melissa. A yearning. One might even go so far as to call it a spark. Something she hadn't allowed herself to feel in years, but now that she had, it wasn't going away. In fact, as the days went on, those feelings were growing stronger.

Now, even though her daughter was still front and centre in her mind, Jane invaded every other thought. She'd somehow made Melissa forget about her ex-husband and how infuriating he could be, and instead, all she could think about was how soft Jane's hand was when she'd held it and whether her lips would be as soft.

Coming to a stop outside The Sweetwater Gazette, Melissa pulled her headphones from her ears and tucked her phone back into her pocket. She pulled her keys out and wrestled the large wooden door open, reminding herself once again to ring someone on Monday about adjusting the hinges.

With a flick of a switch, the room lit up, and Melissa shrugged out of her lightweight jacket, hanging it on the hook. She grabbed the remote for the air conditioner and set it to warm, just enough to take the chill from the early spring air.

This morning's papers had finally gone to print the night before and would now be in mailboxes the town over. A fresh copy lay on her desk beside yesterday's used coffee mug. She swiped the mug Vaughn had painted for her a year ago and took it to the kitchenette to rinse before pouring a fresh coffee. With the rich aroma enticing her nostrils, she sat at her desk, leaning back and pulling the paper towards her. Even after all these years, it still gave her a thrill to see it in print. The name she'd chosen in bold letters across the top, and her own beneath her picture on the inside cover, under the title 'publisher and chief editor'.

She scanned the pages, making sure everything was as it should be, even though she'd done it several times before it went to print. Old habits die hard. When the very first Sweetwater Gazette had gone out, she'd scrutinised every last letter and punctuation mark, every image and column, every advertisement, ensuring it was nothing but perfection. Thirteen years later and nothing had changed. She still proofed each print run cover to cover, still ran her eyes over every aspect of each page. And no matter how many times she did it, she still found satisfaction in the process.

But as she closed the last page and folded the paper in half, she found her mind wandering back to Jane. If the waiter hadn't interrupted them when he did, could something more have happened? Could their innocent hand-holding have turned into something else entirely? If only they'd had just a little more time.

She tapped her finger against the desk, her lips twisted to the side. There would be no harm in reaching out and organising something, would there? Seeing if perhaps there might be more than friendship between them?

On a whim, she pulled her phone from her pocket, and quickly typed out a message asking Jane to keep her company tonight. She pressed send and tucked the phone away before she could overthink it.

She fired her computer up for something to do, bringing up the piece she'd been working on. Aristotle Ballantyne had announced he was stepping down from his mayoral position, and there was much discussion on who would take his place. It was no secret he'd been grooming Lucious for the job, but he'd made it clear his heart wasn't in it, instead opting to start up his own foundation alongside the Sweetwater Youth, where his beau worked. Helping Hands was a place where experienced folk from around the area could come and donate their time to teaching the youth skills to help them in life. Whether it was building a shelf, balancing accounts, or sewing a button on, there was something for everyone. The two places complemented each other perfectly.

But with Lucious no longer in the running, several prominent people had thrown their hats into the ring—including Miranda Baxter and Sandra Smith—along with a few unexpected candidates, and it was looking to be a rather interesting battle of the ballots. Life experience versus fresh blood. Tried and true versus new ideas. Melissa knew where her vote lay.

She busied herself with adding the finishing touches to the piece and slotting images of both the current mayor and the candidates onto the two-page spread. Each candidate had given her a brief bio about themselves along with their plans for the mayoral role. She was in the process of collating their profiles when her phone pinged from her pocket.

With her heart in her throat, she pulled her phone out and swiped the screen.

Jane: You had me at movie and wine. I'm in!

A giddy laugh bubbled out of her mouth as she reread the message. She quickly typed out a response and hit send.

Melissa: It's a date.

Chapter 5

The movie night

"You're pulling my leg, right?" Jane grabbed the remote from Melissa's hand. "That is *not* your favourite movie."

Affronted, Melissa folded her arms across her chest. "It is too. What's wrong with *Labyrinth*?"

"Um, everything." Jane tucked her leg beneath her as she turned to face Melissa. "He's a full-grown man, and she's what? Fifteen? It's creepy." She shuddered. "And don't get me started on those weird things that lose their heads. It's a kids' movie! That's the stuff of nightmares."

Melissa's lips curved up into a grin. "Okay, you make some valid points there, but still, it's David Bowie in tights." She raised her eyebrows with a tilt of her head. "Need I say more?"

"Uh, yeah, I'm going to need more than that. Men in tights don't do it for me."

"Ooh! That's another great movie! I wonder if that's on here." She snatched the remote back and began typing into the search bar. "*Men... in... Tights.*" She let out a sigh. "No."

"What a shame," Jane drawled with a roll of her eyes.

31

Melissa nudged her in the ribs with her elbow. "Okay then, what would be your choice?"

"Oh, that's easy. *Moulin Rouge*."

"Interesting. I didn't have you pegged for a musical theatre type."

"Well, not *all* musical theatre. But that one, most definitely. It has a great soundtrack and hot women in burlesque. Now *that's* what I call entertainment." She swiped her glass of wine from the coffee table, leaning back against the couch with a satisfied grin. "Tell me I'm wrong."

Melissa laughed, pouring another glug of wine into her glass. "You're not wrong." She nodded at the remote. "You choose something then, oh wise one. You clearly have better taste than I do."

Jane's eyebrow rose as she took a sip. "I don't know about that." Her hand fell to the gap between them on the couch, one finger edging close to Melissa's thigh.

Heat pooled in her cheeks, her breath quickening as she let her own hand slide from her lap to the couch. Her eyes were glued to the screen as Jane selected a movie at random, her fingertips a featherlight touch against the back of Melissa's hand.

"5, 6, 7, 8, here we go!" The Onyx Club in Chicago during the 20s appeared on screen. Roxie Hart had her eyes locked on Velma Kelly as she belted out *All that Jazz*.

Jane slid her palm beneath Melissa's, intertwining their fingers as the song came to a crescendo.

Clearing her throat, Melissa croaked, "I love this movie."

"The only other musical theatre I abide." Jane tipped her glass towards the screen. "Again, it's all about the corsets."

"So, they're a prerequisite to you liking a movie?" Melissa asked, a husky tone to her voice. "That's a narrow field."

"I wouldn't say a prerequisite per se. But it definitely gets bonus points if corsets are involved."

Melissa chuckled and, taking a leap of faith, curled her legs on the couch beside her, effectively leaning in closer. Their shoulders pressed together, and Jane sank lower into the cushions, giving her room to slide even closer. She tugged her hand from Melissa's grasp and placed it on her thigh, her fingers tracing back and forth languidly.

"Is this okay?" she whispered, her lips a breath away from the shell of Melissa's ear.

A shiver ran down her back, and she pulled her lip between her teeth, nodding. "Yes."

On the screen, Roxie asked her lover, Fred, to tell her she's a star, and Melissa had never felt she could relate more to a character. When she was younger, Melissa had been a dreamer too, wanting nothing more than to be recognised for her writing. To be a journalistic star, so to speak. Only now, with experience on her side, she knew fame wasn't all it was cracked up to be. She had more joy in the work she did now than she ever did working for the mainstream papers.

She glanced at Jane's hand against her thigh, a smile tugging at her lips. She also found more joy and excitement in knowing Jane than she ever did with Joe by her side. He had been what she thought she wanted and needed at the time, but aside from giving her Vaughn, it was obvious he never could've been the one to make her happy.

This right here, sitting on the couch, curled up with Jane by her side, that was true happiness. That and knowing Vaughn would be back home in the morning.

She let out a contented sigh as she lowered her head to rest on Jane's shoulder, and as she did, Jane wrapped her hand firmly around her inner thigh. The pads of her fingers dug into the soft flesh there, and her thumb dusted lightly across the top of her thigh. Melissa held her breath, silently urging her hand to slide farther up, but at the same time wanting to savour the moment. Once they crossed that line, there was no going back. There would be no more *will she, won't she,* no more anticipation. And wasn't that the best part about falling in love? The anticipation of not knowing?

She stopped herself.

The best part about falling in love…

Was that what this was? Melissa wondered. *Was she falling in love with Jane?*

She thought back over the past few months and how much her life had seemed to blossom with Jane in her orbit. She had finally let someone in, and without even realising it, had allowed herself to fall so deep she couldn't think straight. When something good happened in her life, she wanted to tell Jane, likewise,

34

when her world fell apart, as it had felt like with Joe the other night, it was Jane who came to her rescue. It was Jane who set her world to rights.

What she thought was merely a physical attraction, a scratch she needed to itch, was turning into much more than that. Something deeper and more real than anything she ever had with Joe, and it both scared and exhilarated her. What could be better than falling in love with your best friend?

But then, what could be worse than falling in love with your best friend and having it unrequited? For all she knew, Jane could only be interested in something physical. She never mentioned having a serious relationship. In fact, she tended to avoid those topics altogether, instead focusing on Melissa and her relationship woes. What if Jane wasn't the monogamous type? What if she only wanted a bit of fun? Could she do that and risk her heart breaking?

"What are you thinking about? You've gone all stiff." Jane slid her hand from Melissa's leg and sat up, a worried expression on her face. "Did I go too far?"

"What? No, of course not." She grabbed hold of Jane's hand and placed it back where it was. "I like this." She took a breath, swallowing the lump in her throat. "I like you."

Jane huffed out, something between a laugh and a sigh. "Well that's good then, because I like you too."

"Really?"

Jane tapped her fingers against Melissa's thigh, her eyebrow rising. "Uh, yeah. I thought that was obvious."

Melissa chuckled, dropping her face into her hands. "Ugh, sorry. I was overthinking things. I got inside my own head."

"Believe it or not, that's one of the things I like about you."

Melissa raised her head, a sceptical look on her face. "You're joking."

"Nope." Jane shook her head. "You think things through and don't just jump in headfirst. You're smart and caring, and a great mum." She reached a hand up to cradle Melissa's jaw. "What's not to like?"

"I… um…"

"Don't even try to come up with something. It's too late. I already like you." She grinned, then her eyes flicked to Melissa's lips and back again. Her tongue darted out, wetting her lips as she slowly leaned in. "You can tell me to stop," she whispered, but Melissa shook her head, closing her eyes.

"Don't stop."

Jane's lips were soft as they brushed against hers, and when she pulled back, Melissa let out a whimper. It was all the encouragement Jane needed. Cupping Melissa's jaw in both hands, she pressed her lips to each corner of her mouth, running her tongue along the seam between. Melissa's breath grew ragged as Jane slipped her fingers into the hair at the nape of her neck. Tugging gently, she angled Melissa's head so that her lips fell open in a gasp, an open invitation. Jane kissed her then, their lips melding together as if they were meant for each other.

With their bodies pressed together, Melissa ran her hands up Jane's arms to her shoulders and down to the soft mounds beneath her shirt. Jane sighed against her lips, her back arching, pressing herself against Melissa's touch. Every nerve ending hummed, a song of passion and want. A desire so strong it was almost overwhelming. Melissa couldn't remember a time when she'd been touched like this. It had been far too long, if ever.

Jane reached down to the hem of her top, pulling it over her head and tossing it on the floor. She was exquisite. Lean, flat stomach, pert breasts peeking out beneath a lace bra, and skin soft as silk. Melissa could spend a day trailing her fingers over every curve.

"Your turn." Jane's voice was husky as she peeled Melissa's top from her body and added it to the pile.

Unlike Jane, Melissa was a little softer around the edges. Her stomach still bore the marks of childbirth, though the scars had faded to silver. She stretched her arms above her, showing them off with pride. Jane traced a finger slowly around each one, before lowering her lips to each in turn. When she reached the waistband of Melissa's jeans, she eased them gently down over her hips, until they too were discarded.

"Beautiful," Jane whispered as her eyes drank Melissa in. "So beautiful." She lowered herself down to her elbows, crawling up the length of Melissa's body, every now and then stopping to plant a kiss or trail her tongue along a curve. When she finally settled above her, their breaths were ragged and quick. Crushing her lips to Melissa's, Jane let her hands wander lower, traversing beneath the waistband of her panties. Melissa's breath hitched as Jane curled two fingers, easing them slowly inside.

Melissa's hips bucked of their own volition, her hand reaching down to cover Jane's, urging her on. Together, they moved in sync, their fingers delving and circling until Melissa could barely breathe.

"Oh god!" she cried out as Jane ran her fingers over the sensitive ridge inside. Her hips and thighs seized, and lights danced before her eyes as she fell over the edge and into the abyss.

Jane grinned down at her, catching Melissa's lips in a searing kiss. "You have no idea how long I've wanted to do that."

Chapter 6

The homecoming

"Mum, I'm home!" Vaughn's voice rang out, followed by the front door slamming.

Melissa sat up with a jolt. "Shit!" she hissed, leaping out of bed. Jane was still fast asleep, her blonde hair tousled into a halo around her head. If it wasn't for the sound of Vaughn's heavy booted footsteps thumping across the lounge and down the hall, she'd have taken a moment to take in Jane's dishevelled beauty.

"Mum?"

"Just a sec!" She rushed over to the door and grabbed her robe, flinging it around her shoulders. With a backward glance, she stepped into the hall, pulling the door to behind her. "Hey, sweetheart. Did you have a good time?"

Vaughn threw her bag into her room and sauntered towards Melissa, planting a kiss on her cheek. "It was okay." She scrunched her nose as she took in the dressing gown and bare feet. "Have you only just got up?"

"Ah." Melissa tugged her robe closed around her tightly, running a hand through her hair. She was a notoriously early riser, even on Sundays. "Yeah. Must've slept through my alarm."

39

With a quirk of her brow, Vaughn nodded, a smirk crossing her lips. "Late night, was it?"

Melissa caught her lip between her teeth, suppressing the grin that wanted desperately to escape. While Roxie Hart had learned how *he had it coming,* Jane had been learning the contours of Melissa's body and vice versa. No curve had gone untouched, and they'd spent the night curled around each other. Jane's silky soft skin had been a welcome change to the bobbled flannel sheets she was used to.

Vaughn chuckled. "Do I need to leave and come back again? Give you some alone time?" She made air quotes around the words, a grin splitting her face. She had never seen her mum look so awkward and uncomfortable before.

Melissa, composing herself, pulled herself up to her full five-foot-two height, meeting her daughter's amused gaze. "And what exactly are you insinuating, young lady?"

Vaughn raised a brow. "Ooh, young lady? You *do* have someone in there, don't you?" She glanced to the door to her mother's room with a giddy excitement. "Who is it? Do I know them?"

Floundering, Melissa's mouth gaped open then closed before she collapsed into herself, returning Vaughn's grin. "None of your business."

"Oooh!" Vaughn slapped her hands on her mother's shoulders, pulling her in for a hug. "Go you! It's about time you met someone."

"What's that supposed to mean?"

"It means, you've not been with anyone since Dad, and that's kinda sad. I think it's awesome you're finally getting some."

Melissa screwed her nose up. "I'll have you know, I've been somewhat preoccupied being a mum and entrepreneur. There hasn't been any time for romance."

Vaughn rolled her eyes, tipping her head back and letting out something akin to a snore. "Spare me. I know you've put me first, and I love you for it, but I'm fifteen, Mum. I can look after myself. And The Sweetwater Gazette has been up and running for years now." She spun on her heels, heading down to her room. "I never would've stopped you from seeing anyone before, and I'm not about to now." She swiped her headphones from around her neck and placed them atop her head. When she got to her doorway, she turned and fired a wink at her mother. "I'll be in my room listening to really loud music if you need me."

Melissa shook her head, chuckling. She had definitely put romance on the backburner these past few years, but she didn't realise Vaughn had noticed.

She slipped back into the bedroom, easing the door closed behind her. Jane rolled over, giving her a smile. "Have we been sprung?"

"She knows I have someone here, but she doesn't know it's you." She pulled her lip between her teeth. "I wasn't sure if…" Her face flushed and she averted her eyes.

Jane sat up, pulling the duvet around her and patting the bed. "If I was wanting more than a romp in the hay?"

Melissa grimaced as she perched on the bed beside her. "It sounds bad when you put it that way."

"Uh, yeah, because it is." Jane nudged her in the ribs with her elbow.

"I just mean that I haven't been with anyone since Joe, so I'm out of practice. I don't know what people do these days, you know? Like maybe you just wanted to have some fun and not take it any further—"

Jane stopped her with a kiss to her shoulder. "Stop overthinking things. I told you I like you and not just for your body, damn fine body that it is, but for everything else that you are." She stroked a finger from the shell of Melissa's ear to the base of her neck. "If you'll have me, I'd like to see where this could go."

"Of course I'll have you." She turned, taking Jane's face in the palm of her hand. "It's all I've thought about for the past few weeks." Their lips brushed, a gentle kiss that held a promise of more to come. "Months, if I'm honest."

Jane leaned back, holding the duvet out from her body and peering down at her nakedness. "I mean, I can't say I blame you."

Melissa laughed, swatting her on the arm before collapsing on the bed beside her. She tossed her robe to the floor and dove beneath the blankets, wrapping herself around Jane's sinewy body. A few more moments of bliss before facing the world outside these bedroom walls wouldn't hurt.

Chapter 7

The mural

Vaughn dabbed her brush into the black paint, scraping the excess on the side of the tin. She was almost finished outlining the middle section she'd been working on all week. The vibrant green and blue bubbled text stood out even more with the addition of the black and white accents, and the caricature of Raoul was coming along nicely. She still had to add in drawings of the kids doing various activities, and the famed masks symbolising theatre now that they had done one show and were preparing for another. Giancarlo and Lucious would get a spot somewhere too as they were always hanging out and helping with productions.

Jane bustled through the door wearing a deep red playsuit that clung to her curves and showed off her long legs. Lucious trailed behind her, his hair looking windswept even though the air outside was still. He pushed his sleeves up, nodding a greeting to her.

"Vaughn. That's coming together nicely." He moved to stand behind her, peering over her shoulder. "You've really captured his eyes." He pointed to the large-headed painting of Raoul.

"Thanks. He has kind eyes, so I wanted that to be the focal point. You'll be on there soon too, I hope."

She grinned up at him, waving her paintbrush in his direction. "I think your classic surfer dude hair will be what I focus on for that."

Lucious beamed, running his hand through his blond locks. "It *is* my best feature." He nodded his head towards Jane. "What about the old ball and chain? She get a spot on the wall of fame too?"

"Hey!" Jane slapped a hand against his chest. "I can assure you there are no balls on me whatsoever." She pulled a disgusted face as she waved a hand down the length of her. "This is a ball-free zone."

Vaughn chuckled, nodding her head. "Ball and chain or not, she's still a part of this place, so yeah, she'll get a spot somewhere." She pursed her lips, raking her eyes over Jane's form. "Maybe I'll make the focus on your killer body instead of your face."

Jane snorted. "I don't know whether to be offended you don't like my face or flattered you think I've got a great body." She tossed her hair over her shoulder, threw her hand up to the back of her head and kicked her foot out behind her like one of those pin-up ladies from times gone by. "But you *are* right, it is killer."

Lucious tugged on an imaginary train whistle, saying, "Toot toot," and grinning at her.

"Hey, I'll toot my own damn horn if I want to. If you've got it, flaunt it." She kicked her leg up then dropped the pose, falling into one of the seats at the table. "Seriously though, Vaughn. This is looking stellar. I can't believe you won't let your mum see it yet. You know she just wants to fawn over you and tell you how proud she is."

Vaughn rolled her eyes. "Which is exactly why I don't want her to see it yet. She can fawn all over the finished product. Like everyone else." She'd already spoken to Raoul about sectioning it off to keep it a surprise. Shane and Adrian were meant to be jacking something up for her soon. Pursing her lips, Vaughn tucked the paintbrush behind her ear and swivelled around to stand with her hip cocked and arms folded across her chest. "Speaking of my mum. You guys have become pretty close, right? Do you know who she was shacked up with over the weekend?"

Jane sucked in a breath then coughed, thumping a hand against her chest. Lucious looked on with an amused expression, as if he knew more than he was letting on. Vaughn raised her eyes to him, but he waved her away. "I don't know anything."

"Have you asked her?" Jane said. "It's really not my place to go around telling her secrets."

Vaughn placed a hand to her chest. "I'm not just anyone. I'm her daughter. We don't keep secrets from each other."

"Then you can hear it from her, can't you? I'm not about to divulge anything without talking to her first."

Vaughn's shoulders sagged and she pouted. "Spoil sport."

"I'm sure she'd tell you if she was ready to. Maybe she wants to feel it out first before saying anything."

"Yeah," Lucious cut in. "Sometimes parents don't like introducing a new love interest to their children until they're sure where it's headed. Maybe leave it a week or two. Let her come to you."

Jane turned to him with a surprised expression. "Wise words."

He laughed, shoving his hand in the pocket of his jean shorts. "I have been known to have the odd wise moment. It doesn't happen often, but it does happen."

"What does?" Raoul asked, stepping up beside Lucious and planting a kiss to his cheek.

"Lucious is just telling us how he's not just a pretty face with perfect hair, he's actually smart sometimes too." Jane said matter-of-factly before sticking her tongue out at him. "He's the whole package."

"You joke, but I haven't heard Raoul complain once."

"And you won't hear me complain either. Unless it's about the wet towels he leaves on the floor beside the basket instead of in it." He pointed a finger to Lucious's chest, which he grabbed and used to pull him flush against his body.

"I don't know why it bothers you so much, it's not like you do the washing." He grinned, tipping his head to his beau. "Roberta doesn't seem to mind."

Raoul feigned shock, placing a hand to his heart. "You'd rather let a woman old enough to be your grandmother stoop down to pick up your soiled clothes than put them in the basket for her?" He shook his head, tsking. "I'm seeing you in a whole new light, Lucious Ballantyne."

"Ooh, you got the full name treatment. That's never good." Vaughn stifled her laugh behind her hand. "Someone's in trouble," she sang as she turned back to the wall and her partially-done masterpiece. She added another swipe of black along the length of the exclamation point following Sweetwater Youth, then grabbed another brush and added a sparkle of white on the inside curve.

Raoul placed a hand on her shoulder, giving it a squeeze. "It's looking great, Vaughn. Just what this place needed." He pointed to the image of his likeness. "Though I don't see why I'm the one front and centre when it's you who's doing all the work."

Vaughn rolled her eyes. "Fishing for compliments is so not cool," she said with a smirk. "But if I have to spell it out, I will." She turned her gaze to him. "You're like the glue that holds this place together, or whatever." She rolled her eyes again, huffing, as if it took great pains to admit it.

Raoul chuckled. "Thanks for the vote of confidence."

"Anytime, boss man." She waved her hands, shooing them away. "Now let me get back to work while the light is still good."

Chapter 8

The new dynamic

"So, I was at the youth centre this afternoon, and Vaughn was asking me who you were with in the weekend." Jane popped a carrot stick into her mouth, then wiped her fingers on a serviette. She grabbed the platter with hummus, crackers and sliced veggies, carrying it through to the living room.

Melissa stood in the doorway, a bowl of popcorn balanced precariously between her hip and elbow. "What did you tell her?"

Jane shrugged. "I told her she needs to talk to you about that."

"Does it bother you that I haven't told her yet?"

"Of course not. It's only been a few days. I'm not expecting you to shout your undying love for me from the rooftops until at least a week has gone past. Two at the most. Anything past that and..." She shook her head with a sigh. "I just don't know how I'll feel about that." Her brow furrowed briefly before the corners of her mouth lifted and she let out a snort. "Relax, Mel. She's your daughter. Only you can know when it's right to tell her. I'm not about to say how and when you do anything."

Melissa's shoulders sagged with relief. Being with Jane was considerably different to being with Joe.

He was one of those men who believed they knew best for everyone. It would have killed him to have her deny him to anyone. It was his way, or no way at all.

Jane was so easy going and open to whatever came her way. It was refreshing.

"Are you going to just stand there all night? Because the movie is like three hours long and that could get uncomfortable." She scooched back against the couch, tucking her legs beneath her. "But, you know, whatever. You do you, boo."

Melissa stifled a laugh and added the popcorn to the coffee table already laden with snacks and drinks, then grabbing the doorframe, she swung her body into it, hollering down the hall, "Movie's about to start!"

"Be there in a minute!" came the muffled reply from behind Vaughn's closed door. She'd been doing that a lot lately; keeping her door closed. Melissa knew it was par for the course with having a teenage daughter, but still, it saddened her that she was shutting herself away more these days. They used to spend so much time hanging out together. Now, she had to take what she could get.

Padding over to the couch, Melissa took up the spot next to Jane, a hairsbreadth between their thighs. She could feel the warmth radiating from her body, and she wanted so much to snuggle in close and rest her head on her shoulder, but it was too soon. As much as she enjoyed Jane's company, she had to tread carefully around Vaughn. She'd heard all too many times how many women her father had introduced her to over the years, and just how much she hated it. She was tired of getting to know them and then finding someone had replaced them the next time she visited. And though Melissa saw this thing with Jane going somewhere, she wasn't ready to introduce her into her daughter's life as 'another one who could leave'. After Joe's last relationship busted up, Vaughn had been devastated. She'd gotten to know Sandy quite well over the months, and there'd even been talk of wedding bells and her being the maid of honour. It had taken a lot of coaxing to get her to come out of her room and talk about it.

It broke Melissa's heart to see her hurting over the loss of her almost step-mother, and she couldn't bear it if she was the one to cause that same pain this time around. Taking things slowly was the only way this was going to work.

"Ooh popcorn." Vaughn uplifted the bowl, taking it with her to the chair beside the couch. She plonked herself down, draping a throw across her lap and cradling the bowl against her. "Ready."

Jane watched her with a quirked brow. "I am shooketh. I did not see you as a popcorn hog." She lunged forward, snatching up the bowl of chips and settling it between her and Melissa. "Two can play at that game."

Vaughn snorted around her mouthful. "No skin off my nose, man. I can smell the disgusting vinegar flavour from here." She scrunched her face. "Gross."

Pointing a chip at Vaughn, Jane said, "You, my dear, are a heathen. Salt and vinegar chips are divine. They're only the best flavour on the planet, and I'll not hear otherwise." She folded her arms across her chest with a huff.

"Easy, tiger. You can have all the salt and vinegar chips you like, just keep them away from me." She raised her bowl of popcorn. "I'm good with this."

Melissa couldn't help but smile at the playful banter between the two most important women in her life. And she hoped beyond anything that she didn't fuck this thing up with Jane, for both their sakes.

The screen lit up with a view of the ocean then diving deep below the surface to where the ruins of the Titanic lay.

After a few minutes, Vaughn spoke up. "It doesn't make sense."

"What doesn't?"

She pointed at the screen, her eyes locked on the crackly images of the sunken ship. "That. I mean, I know it happened, and I know it's real, but how can the ocean be *that* deep that an entire ship is just sitting there like that. Like, it's one big ship burial ground, and we can't even see it from the surface. You have to dive down so deep to see it." She turned to them with awe. "Like how is that even possible?"

Melissa smiled. This was what she'd been missing. The kind of conversations only Vaughn could come up with. "It's hard to wrap your head around it, right? I guess the ocean is vaster than we really comprehend."

"It's kinda scary, don't you think? Like, if a whole ship can be so far below, what else is down there?" She popped another piece of popcorn into her mouth, turning back to the screen to see Rose begin her story.

"If Disney and Pixar movies have taught me anything, it's that the sea is full of weird and wonderful things," Jane added, pausing the movie.

Vaughn made a half-cough half-snort noise in the back of her throat. "You watch kids' movies?"

Affronted, Jane placed a hand to her chest. "I'm a kid at heart."

"Mmhmm. All the kids these days wear pantsuits." Vaughn chuckled, tossing a piece of popcorn at Jane.

"Alright. Okay, Miss Thang. You do not get to criticise what I wear when kids of your generation have chosen to bring back mullets and high-waisted jeans. Those things belong back in the 80s where they came from."

"I see your point, and I agree. You'll never see me sporting a mullet or jeans pulled so high you can see what I ate for lunch. No thank you."

Jane barked out a laugh. "Good to hear, kid. I wouldn't want to have to lecture you on the unnecessary thing that is a camel toe."

"Ewww!" Vaughn ducked her head beneath the blanket. "Is she done yet?"

Laughing, Melissa gripped the corner of the blanket and tugged. "Yes, the crazy lady is done being vulgar. Right, Jane?"

She raised her hands in placation. "Okay, fine. No more camel toe talk from me." She ran her fingers across her lips in a zipping motion. "My lips are sealed. Both sets."

Vaughn looked mortified, and this time, Melissa couldn't contain her laughter. "Stop, or she'll never want to watch a movie with us again."

"It's a life lesson she needs to learn. Just like Lucious had to when he bought those hideous tan slacks that were a size too small just so he could have his bare ankles exposed. Believe me, that moose had some knuckles on it."

Melissa pursed her lips, but her laughter forced its way out, and she threw her head against the back of the couch as she swiped tears from her eyes. "Oh my god."

"Honestly, I had to make Raoul talk to him about it, because he wasn't listening to me." She leaned in, holding her hand to her mouth as an aside. "Though, between you and me, I think Raoul secretly liked it. They probably use them for a bit of roleplay in the bedroom." She waggled her brows suggestively.

"No!" Vaughn clapped her hands over her ears. "That's my youth leader you're talking about." She scrunched her eyes closed. "La la la, I can't hear you."

"You've scarred her for life now. She'll never be able to look Raoul or Lucious in the eyes again." Melissa chuckled, her pinkie finger wrapping around Jane's beneath the bowl of chips. This right here was what she needed in her life. Hanging out with her daughter, having a few laughs, and all with Jane by her side.

Chapter 9

The close call

Soft lips brushed against Melissa's brow, then her cheek, and finally her mouth. She rolled over with a smile on her face, wrapping her arms around Jane and snuggling in close. "Morning." Her voice was groggy with sleep.

"Morning," Jane whispered, slipping out from her grasp.

Melissa blinked against the filtered light streaming through the net curtains, her eyes landing on the bold red numbers of her alarm clock. She jolted upright. "Shit, it's 7:30," she hissed, throwing back the blankets and swinging her feet to the floor.

Jane chuckled low in her throat. "Don't worry about it. Her door is still shut. I'll just slip out through the kitchen. She won't even know I'm here." She tugged her navy turtleneck over her head, flicking her hair out from beneath the cuff. "I may not look it, but I can be stealthy."

Melissa took in her long, slender legs and the graceful way she moved. There was no doubt in her mind she could be surreptitious when she wanted to be. Still, she hated having to make her sneak around like what they were doing was wrong.

"You don't have to look so miserable. I'll come back tonight if you want me to." Jane traipsed over, pulling her into her arms.

"It's not that."

"Harsh."

Melissa tapped her fingers playfully against Jane's arms. "You know that's not what I meant. You're welcome here anytime. It's just…" She shifted her gaze to the door. "I hate that I'm making this difficult on you with all the clandestine operations going on."

"Are you kidding? It's taking me back to my youth." Jane grinned, her tongue poking between her teeth. "It's like all those times I was sneaking out behind my parents' backs, only this time I can't get grounded."

"You're actually enjoying this?" Melissa shook her head, untangling her limbs from Jane's. "I should've known."

"You can't tell me it doesn't make you feel younger." She swatted Melissa's bottom as she turned to grab her robe and drape it across her shoulders.

Melissa tried but failed to hide her smile. "Okay, fine. It does make me feel a little younger." She held her thumb and forefinger in the air to demonstrate just how little she meant. "Come on, I'll walk you out before the 'parentals' wake." She held her finger to her lips as she eased the door open.

Tiptoeing quickly down the hall, they made it into the kitchen, only to stop short at the sight of Vaughn sitting at the counter with a bowl of cereal in front of her. They jumped apart, Melissa wrapping her robe tighter around her body as Vaughn turned to face them.

"Morning. You here for breakfast, Jane?" She shook a box of Fruit Loops in the air. "We have plenty." She turned back to her bowl, not even batting an eye.

Melissa cleared her throat, stepping into the kitchen and planting a kiss on her daughter's head. "Ah yeah, that's why she's here. Right, Jane?" She gave her an imploring look, and Jane jumped right into character.

"That's right. When I left last night, we made plans to have breakfast together. Only sleeping beauty over there slept in." She took up the stool beside Vaughn, snaffling the cereal box off the counter and taking a handful.

Vaughn shifted her gaze to her mother. "See? It's not uncouth. Jane does it too." She swiped the box and tipped a handful into her own palm, nudging her bowl aside. "The milk makes all the flavours mix together and you don't get the individual tastes. Just like with Skittles. You have to savour each flavour." She rolled her eyes, turning to Jane. "I've been trying to tell her this for ages, but she *insists* I pour milk in with them." She turned her nose up at the bowl.

"Oh, Mel." Jane tutted, shaking her head. "This is the *only* way to appreciate Fruit Loops."

"Oh, I see how it is. We're ganging up on me now?" She dragged the half-eaten bowl of cereal across the counter and grabbed the spoon. "Cereal is meant to be eaten with milk. Look on the box." She pointed the spoon at the front of the package, where a toucan sat gazing at a bowl of milky cereal.

"Hmmm. I don't know." Jane tipped three purple loops into her mouth, chewing thoughtfully. "Looks to me like they're trying to escape the bowl of milk."

Melissa laughed, her eyes dancing. "Stop encouraging her."

"Hey, I'm only speaking the truth. Have you even *tried* them without milk?"

"No, she hasn't." Vaughn grinned, enjoying watching her mother squirm. "She flat out refuses."

"Well…" Jane pushed up from her seat, rounding the counter. "How can you possibly know unless you try?" With her eyes locked on Melissa's, she fished inside the box, pulling out a small handful. She held a green one between her thumb and finger. "Open wide."

Melissa acquiesced, her lips falling open. Jane pushed the loop slowly into her mouth. "Roll it around on your tongue. Savour every taste." Her voice was sensual, and the way she was watching Melissa's lips had her cheeks warming. "Now the red one." Another burst of flavour exploded on her tongue.

"It's good, right?" Vaughn piped up.

Melissa swallowed, turning back to the bowl of cereal that now held little appeal. Not after being handfed by Jane. She couldn't bring herself to raise the spoon to her lips, instead, she pushed the bowl aside.

Vaughn grinned triumphantly, high-fiving Jane. "I knew it!"

"And that, my dear, is your lesson for the day," Jane said. "You're never too old to try new things."

Chapter 10

The shopping expedition

"We really need Raoul here. He's much better at picking out fashionable clothes than I am." Jane plucked at the oversized crimson sweatshirt that hung off one shoulder, exposing creamy white skin. She'd paired it with a pair of blue jeans that looked as if they'd been painted on, and black ankle boots.

"Yeah," Melissa deadpanned. "You have no style at all. You need to take a leaf out of my book." She held her hands out to the side and did a pirouette. "I see your skinny jeans and raise you a pair of torn, stained mum jeans, complete with street shoes and a hoodie." She swiped non-existent dust from her shoulder. "It takes a special someone to pull off this look."

Vaughn slipped between them, linking her arms with theirs. "If we're competing for the best dress sense, then I've got this one in the bag." She kicked her leg up, waving one foot in the air. "Chunky black boots with distressed black jeans trumps them all. And, of course, I've got the green hair to make a statement." She flicked her head, but not a hair moved there was so much product holding it in place. Today she had it parted to the side, with one section braided against her scalp, and the other split into thick strands. Where she got her fashion sense from was something Melissa often wondered, because it clearly wasn't from her or Joe. She had a style all of her own.

"What exactly are we looking for again?" Melissa asked her daughter as they strolled past several stores on the main stretch of road through town.

Vaughn scrunched her nose. "They *want* us to wear something feminine and pretty, but…" She stuck her tongue out, making a gagging sound. "No thank you."

"Couldn't you just put your own style into it? Wear a frock with your Doc Martens?" Melissa suggested.

"That's actually very in right now," Jane agreed. "And if anyone can pull that look off, it's you… and Madonna, maybe Cyndi Lauper too." Jane pursed her lips, tilting her head towards the sky as she tried to recall her childhood.

They stopped outside Giancarlos, and Vaughn looked at the mannequins in the window. "I had something a little more like this in mind." She sucked her lips between her teeth and peered at her mother. "Is that okay?"

"Of course it is. It's your school formal. You can wear whatever you like, honey." She pushed the door open, a little bell ringing as they stepped across the threshold.

"Jane, Vaughn," Giancarlo greeted, stepping out from behind the counter. "To what do I owe the pleasure?" His eyes danced across her companions, a smirk playing across his lips.

Jane placed her hands on Vaughn's shoulders. "We're here to find a suit for this one. Got anything that'll fit?"

Giancarlo looked at her as if she'd said the most preposterous thing in the world. "My dear, I'm insulted you even have to ask." He waved a hand around the store. "Whatever the lovely Vaughn desires, I can alter it to fit, or I can wrangle up a one-of-a-kind piece just for her." He winked at Vaughn. "What do you say?"

Her eyes lit up as she turned to Melissa. "Can I?"

A one-of-a-kind Giancarlo piece would cost a fortune, but it was worth it to see that smile on her face. "Of course, honey." She would take it up with Joe later, see if he could put something towards it.

Giancarlo wrapped his arm around Vaughn's shoulders, leading her towards the counter. He pulled out a pad of paper and a pencil and began to jot down her ideas.

Raoul poked his head out from the back room. "Oh, hey you two. I thought I heard familiar voices." His eyes seemed to zip around the room expectantly, and Jane snorted.

"He's not here. I'm playing hookie. Don't tell Lucious." She whispered the last part, placing her finger to her lips.

Raoul folded his arms across his chest, a look of disappointment on his face. "Now why would you go and put me in that kind of position?"

"I'm joking. He knows all about it." She nodded over to where Vaughn was animatedly describing something that looked like a long tail, and Giancarlo

63

was nodding, his fingers flying across the paper. "And we're here for her. I'm sure you know formal season is coming up."

His eyebrows shot up, but he nodded. "That makes perfect sense, actually. I was wondering what she'd end up going with. Ballgowns just don't seem like a Vaughn thing."

Melissa shook her head. "No, they never have been really. Even as a little girl she would choose pants over dresses, and you'd never catch her in those sparkly sandals or high heels. It was gumboots or sneakers." She laughed. "I've never known anyone besides Vaughn to wear a pair of gumboots so often the soles wore down."

"I'm glad she graduated from gumboots to Doc Martens. Could you imagine her walking around home with those squeaky things on all the time? And she'd never be able to sneak out at night either. Wait." Jane tapped her chin. "Maybe that's a good thing. Vaughn, what do you think about a pair of gumboots to go with it?" she called out.

Giancarlo looked appalled, but Vaughn looked as though she was considering it before scrunching her nose up. "That's a hard pass."

Jane shrugged. "It was worth a shot."

Melissa patted her arm. "Your heart was in the right place."

"Thank Christ for that. Wouldn't want it galivanting off to places unknown."

64

Melissa snorted, and Raoul looked on with amusement. He caught Jane's gaze and raised a brow. She simply grinned.

"Mum, have a look. What do you think?" Vaughn thrust the notepad in front of her. While they'd been talking, Giancarlo had sketched out an entire outfit, complete with colours and fabric styles. Charcoal pants cut off below her shins to allow her to wear her favourite pair of boots. A pastel green shirt, cinched in at the waist, and a charcoal jacket with satin edging and tails to wear over top. A small green pocket square and bow tie finished it off.

"Wow, that's going to be quite some suit." She took hold of Vaughn's hand, giving it a squeeze. "I'm happy if you're happy."

Vaughn stared down at the image in a dreamlike trance. "It's better than I could've imagined." When she looked up at Giancarlo, there was a glassiness to her eyes, and Melissa's heart jolted. This was important to her.

"Then I guess we'd better get it then."

Giancarlo nodded, tugging the measuring tape from around his neck. "Let's get you measured up, my dear."

Chapter 11

The conversation

"So, the other weekend, when I was at Dad's…" Vaughn tilted her head and pursed lips. "It was Jane in your room, wasn't it?"

Melissa inhaled sharply, then coughed as a trickle of water went down wrong.

"And you're like together? Like more than friends?"

She should have known Vaughn would figure it out before she was ready for this conversation. She always was a smart girl, and they hadn't exactly been discrete. Jane was here almost every night. Still, even though she expected it, it didn't make having this conversation any easier. It was still early days, and she and Jane had barely even scratched the surface of what they were together.

Vaughn thumped her mum on the back, rubbing in circles as she coughed a few more times.

"Sorry," Melissa spluttered, placing a hand to her chest as she cleared her throat again. She met Vaughn's gaze with a sheepish grin. "Uh, yeah, we are. Is… is that okay with you?" She spread her hands across the counter in front of her, the cool, smooth surface grounding her. It hadn't occurred to her until now that

67

Vaughn might not be okay with it, and she didn't know what she would do if that were the case.

Vaughn snorted, a grin spreading across her lips. "Uh, yeah, of course it's okay. Don't look so worried." She gave her a sideways glance. "Didn't have you pegged for a cougar though."

"What? I am not." *Am I?* "I'm only five years older—"

Vaughn chuckled. "Relax, Mum. I was joking."

Melissa huffed out a sigh of relief. "I know it probably comes as a bit of a shock to you, seeing me with a woman, and a *younger* woman at that—"

"Not really," Vaughn interrupted. "I had my suspicions after the show."

"You did?"

"Yeah. You should've seen your face when you saw her. It lit up."

Melissa smiled at the memory, her fingertips trailing across her cheeks.

"I think it's kinda cool actually."

"You do?"

Vaughn nodded. "Yup." Her lips twisted to the side. She trailed a finger across the counter then glanced up at her mother. "It makes way more sense than you and Dad did. He's so stuffy—"

Melissa tutted, folding her arms across her chest. "He's still your father and you shouldn't speak about him that way."

Vaughn smirked. "You do."

An abrupt laugh fell from Melissa's lips. Caught out. "You're not meant to hear those conversations."

"Then you shouldn't speak so loudly." Vaughn grinned. "It's true though. Jane is much more laid back and your style. She's cool. I like her."

"Well good then. I like her too." She smiled, turning to the fridge and pulling out the makings of a salad for dinner.

"I just, ya know, wanted you to know I'm cool with it, and you don't have to pretend or anything. Like I'm okay with her being here when I'm here."

Melissa concentrated on the lettuce leaves she was shredding as she reigned in the tears forming in her eyes. It meant everything to have Vaughn's approval. She hadn't let herself feel anything romantic towards anyone since Joe left, and it felt good to finally take down that barrier she'd built around herself.

"And…" Vaughn cleared her throat then let out a long, drawn-out breath, as if preparing herself for something huge.

Melissa glanced up at her daughter, seeing the way she fidgeted in her seat and couldn't meet her eyes. She put the lettuce down on the chopping board, drying her hands on a dish towel. "Is everything okay?" She rounded the counter to stand beside Vaughn, leaning her hip on the cool granite.

"Mmhmm." Vaughn nodded, but her lips were pulled to the side as she chewed the inside of her mouth. She hadn't done that since she was young.

"Whatever you want to say, honey, I'm here." She took her daughter's chin in her hand, stroking her thumb along the silky soft skin of her cheek. "You can tell me anything."

"I know." She paused. "I want to, I just don't know *how* to say it."

"You have more questions about me and Jane?"

She shook her head. "No, it's not that."

"Your dad? School?"

"No, well, not really. I don't know, maybe?" She squinted her eyes and brought a hand up to run through her bright green hair. "It's just that, um… I know Dad doesn't like the way I dress, and I know he won't like that we bought a suit for the formal…"

"He doesn't have to like it. It's you who's wearing it."

"But it's so expensive, and I know we can't afford it."

"Hey, you're going to look stunning in that suit. You'll wow the pants off everyone there, mark my words." She brushed her hand across Vaughn's cheek. "You let me worry about the money, okay? Is that all that's bothering you?"

Vaughn's eyes watered and she shook her head. "Why won't he call me Vaughn like everyone else does? I've told him I don't feel like a Siobhan, but he ignores me."

Melissa's chest tightened. She knew she should've pushed harder with Joe to listen to what Vaughn wanted. "I'm sorry, baby. He can be stubborn. Let me talk to him again."

Vaughn nodded. "Okay… Um, there's something else too. And I don't think he'll like this either." She swallowed, and her knee bobbed up and down repeatedly.

"Okay?" She drew out the word, unsure whether to be worried or not.

"Um… It's something I've been thinking about for a while now, and I've already told my friends." She glanced up sheepishly. "I think, at least, I *hope* you'll get it more now that you're with Jane…"

Realisation dawned, and Melissa kicked herself for not paying more attention. "Are you saying you like girls too? Is that it?"

Vaughn's cheeks reddened and she ducked her head. "I don't really know what I like, if that makes sense." She peeked up at her mother. "But… um… you know how I don't really feel like a Siobhan?"

Melissa nodded.

"Well, I don't really feel like I fit into the box of…" She took a breath. "Of being… a girl either." She winced, as if expecting harsh words to come her way, but all Melissa wanted to do was wrap her arms around her daughter and offer her comfort, and she did. She wrapped her arms so tightly around Vaughn, that there could be no misunderstanding of how she felt.

When they pulled apart, Vaughn looked up at Melissa. "I don't really feel like I fit in any box."

"That's okay, honey." She cupped Vaughn's jaw, tilting their face to meet her gaze. "Fitting into a box is overrated anyway. You are who you are, and whoever that ends up being is okay with me." She kissed them on the head. "Do you want me to talk to your father about it?"

Vaughn wiped a tear from their cheek and smiled. "No. I think I can do it. I just needed to know you were on my side first."

"Of course I am. I'm always on your side. No matter what."

Chapter 12

The weekend

"Melissa. You're looking well." Joe nodded as he stood stiffly in the doorway. "I wondered if we might have a word?" He gestured for her to join him outside.

"Ah, sure. I actually need to have a word with you too." She stepped out into the cool air, the sky already turning a dusky shade of orange as the sun sank below the horizon.

Joe cleared his throat, obviously uncomfortable with whatever he needed to broach, and Melissa was automatically on edge.

"Just spit it out, Joe." She wrapped her arms around herself, not only to combat the cold, but to brace herself for what he was about to say. If it was making him this uncomfortable, it couldn't be good.

"I don't mean to alarm you, but I felt you ought to know what people have been saying about you." He rolled his shoulders, brushing his hands down the front of his tailored jacket.

"About me?"

"Indeed." He nodded solemnly. "It's somewhat of a personal nature."

"Stop beating around the bush and just come out with it."

"Well that's the thing. They're saying you've—" he lowered his voice, "—come out of the closet and are seeing a woman."

"Right." She drew the word out. "And?"

"What do you mean and? Isn't that enough on its own?" He frowned. "It's not… it's not true, is it?"

Melissa crooked her brow, folding her arms across her chest. "As a matter of fact, it is true, and before you ask, Vaughn is fine with it."

"Siobhan knows?" His gaze darkened. "You think that's wise?"

Melissa snorted. "That's rich, coming from you."

"Excuse me?"

"How many women have you introduced Vaughn to over the years? A hell of a lot more than one, that's for sure."

"It's hardly the same thing."

"Isn't it?"

"Of course not."

"Well, that's your opinion. I'm happy, and so is Vaughn. That's all that should matter to you."

He scoffed, shaking his head and muttering to himself.

"Now, I need to ask you for a little extra this month. The school formal is coming up, and Vaughn has chosen a suit from Giancarlos."

Joe folded his arms across his chest, widening his stance. "Giancarlos is high-end menswear. He doesn't cater to women and ballgowns."

"I know that. I said Vaughn wants to wear a suit, not a dress. It's already designed, and Giancarlo is doing me a good deal on it."

"And this is your doing too, I suppose?"

Melissa huffed out a sigh. "This has nothing to do with me or Jane, if that's what you're insinuating. Vaughn is more than capable of making their own mind up."

"As am I, and I'm not about to pay for my daughter to go to her formal dressed like a man. You want my help to pay for a gown, fine, but I'll not have any part in this ridiculousness."

"Fine," Melissa gritted out.

"Excellent." He pulled out his cheque book. "What's the going rate for a gown these days?"

Melissa placed her hand over his, pushing it away. "I mean fine, I don't need your money. I'll sort it out myself."

"Don't be stupid, Melissa."

"I'm not. I'm giving Vaughn the support they need. You should try it sometime." She spun on her heels, striding for the door just as Vaughn stepped out.

"Mum?"

Forcing a smile to her lips, Melissa gripped her daughter's arms and pulled them in for a hug. "Everything's fine, honey. Have a great time. I'll miss you."

Vaughn snorted. "No you won't. You've got Jane to keep you company now." They grinned.

"Yes, I do, but she'll never replace you."

"I know, Mum. That would be gross if she did."
They scrunched their nose, poking their tongue out.

Joe stalked to the car, wrenching the door open.
"Come on, Siobhan. I haven't got all night."

Melissa clenched her jaw, one of her eyelids
ticking as she tried not to react. "You'd better get going
before he blows a fuse."

"Did you ask him about the suit?"

Pressing her lips into a thin line, she nodded. "I
did."

Vaughn's face dropped. "Oh."

"Don't worry about it. I'll make it work. You go
and have a good time." She stepped back onto the
welcome mat, watching as Vaughn climbed into the
passenger seat. The engine stirred to life, and Vaughn
waved until the car was all the way out onto the road.
Melissa stood there, her arms curling around her for
comfort. Getting through to Joe was going to prove
difficult.

Chapter 13

The double date

The air was crisp as Jane tugged on Melissa's hand, dragging her towards Helping Hands. "Are you sure about this? I thought it was meant to be for the kids."

"Of course I'm sure. Lucious invited us himself, and he's the one running the show." She spun on her heel, walking backwards along the path so she could give Melissa puppy-dog eyes. "Come on, it'll be fun."

"Okay, but if you start singing *Unchained Melody* and coating my arms in clay, I'm outta there."

Jane pouted. "You're no fun. How can we possibly spin a vase without re-enacting it? I feel like... no, I'm *certain* it's illegal to go to a pottery class and *not* do it."

Laughing, Melissa shook her head. "Maybe if it was just the two of us. I know Vaughn is okay with it, but I'm not sure I'm ready to go full on PDA in front of a class of strangers."

Jane fell into step beside her. "Not all of them are strangers. Raoul and Lucious will be there too, remember? That's how a double date works."

Melissa pinned her with a stare. "That's worse! It's bad enough I'm going to be picturing Lucious in his moose knuckle pants and the two of them role playing. I'm not about to scar them with an equally damaging image of the two of us rolling around in a puddle of clay."

"Oh come on, they'll love it. It'll be the highlight of their night. Their week even." Jane grinned. "I bet they'll even be jealous they didn't think of it first."

"You don't think two men who helped put on the first theatre show this town has seen in years, won't have instantly thought of the most iconic romantic moment involving clay in cinematic history? You're dreaming." Amusement danced in Melissa's eyes; a welcome change to how she'd felt earlier in the evening. Hell, perhaps she should let Jane play out her *Ghost* fantasy. It'd certainly keep the anger at bay, at least until Sunday night when she'd have to face Joe again. No doubt he'll have a thing or two to say, if Vaughn manages to talk to him, that is. She didn't envy them that challenge. And challenge it would be. She still couldn't fathom how she hadn't realised how small-minded and shallow he could be when they were together. It's a wonder they survived as long as they did.

They rounded the corner where the Sweetwater Youth met each day. Lights shone out from the window, and kids of all ages sat around tables playing board games or doing homework, while others looked to be making a video on their phones. Melissa had to fight to keep her eyes affixed on the children and not the mural Vaughn was working on. She wanted so much to see how it was going, but she'd made a promise that she wouldn't look until Vaughn was finished.

Jane nudged her in the ribs. "You should see the way they've depicted you on it."

"What?" She turned her attention to Jane, her eyes wide with shock.

Jane's brow creased. "You didn't know?"

"Of course I didn't kn—"

Jane grinned, her tongue poking between her teeth.

"Oh, ha ha, very funny." She jostled Jane with her elbow.

"Stopped you from peeking though, didn't it?" She waggled her brows. "Not that you'd see anything anyway. It's all covered up now. Not even Raoul is allowed to see it."

Knowing the man who'd given them the task wasn't allowed to see it either made her feel slightly better. She could wait a little longer.

They carried on to the next block. Having the mayor as your father had its perks. When Lucious had embarked on his Helping Hands plan, Aristotle had pulled a few strings to get him a building within walking distance of the youth centre. Raoul could often be spotted leading a gang of kids down to the workshops held in the evenings.

Lucious greeted them at the door with a welcome smile. "You made it. Come in, come in." He stepped back, waving his arm out. "Raoul's already inside." He pushed the door closed, shoving his hand in his pocket and falling into step beside them. "Angelique has a workshop with the kids tomorrow, so we have the place to ourselves tonight."

"Ooh, cosy," Jane quipped.

"I didn't realise it was an additional class. I thought we were joining in on one. How nice of her to give up her evening for us." Melissa shrugged her coat off, handing it to Lucious. "We should've bought her some wine or something."

"Already taken care of." Lucious winked, draping her jacket across the back of a chair as he sauntered past. He slinked his arm around Raoul. "Look who I found."

"Ladies, nice of you to join us." He tilted his head.

"And this lovely lady is Angelique Moriarty. She runs Potty for Pottery on the main road out to Dursey." He wrapped an arm around the woman's shoulders like they were old friends. Angelique had long chestnut coloured hair with flecks of silver around the temples. Her kind eyes crinkled when she smiled up at Lucious.

"Oh, that cute boutique store on the way to Chefield?" Melissa asked, and Angelique nodded with a warm smile. "I love that place."

"How very kind of you to say, thank you." She folded her hands in front of her. "It's been a real passion project for me."

"I don't doubt it. The pieces you make are exquisite." Melissa turned to Jane. "There was this peacock that stood about this high—" she hovered her hand by her waist, "—with gorgeously painted tail feathers in full spread." She shook her head in awe. "It was beautiful. And the handcrafted dinnerware…" She held a hand to her chest. "Breath-taking."

80

Angelique laughed, a light and airy sound. "You really are a fan, aren't you? Makes tonight even more special." She gestured to the chunks of clay in front of them. "Shall we?" She placed her hand over the clump, letting her fingers squish into it. "Take a hold of the clay. Feel it in your hands. Try and envisage what it could be." Her fingers kneaded the earthen material, making it more pliable. "And when you're ready, move over to your pottery wheel." Dropping the clay to the surface, she dipped her hands into a bowl of water nearby. Her fingers glided over the clay, caressing it as the table spun slowly.

Jane gave Melissa a knowing look as she perched behind her wheel. Unbidden, the lyrics of *Unchained Melody* began playing through her mind, and she had to stifle her laugh.

Beside her, Lucious began to hum the very same tune beneath his breath, almost as if he didn't realise he was doing it. Jane snorted, and Melissa could barely contain her mirth. She pressed her lips into a thin line, trying to focus on the clay before her, but Lucious, noticing their reaction, kicked it up a notch. He sucked in a breath before belting out a loud and long "Whoa," before Jane joined in with the next line.

Raoul chuckled, but his eyes remained fixed on the task at hand. He already had the makings of a small bowl forming, which was more than the rest of them could say. Jane's had caved in when she started singing, and Lucious's hadn't made it past the blob stage. Melissa had created a short, lop-sided cylinder, but she hadn't hollowed it out as yet.

At the front of the room, Angelique had a Mona Lisa smile on her face as her hands moulded the clay on the wheel, slowly turning what was once a chunk of earth into a beautiful, ornate vase with rippling edges that curved outwards. Her fingers continued to glide over and work the clay, extending the length and adding more detail. It was mesmerising to watch.

Seeming to snap out of her reverie, Angelique glanced up, peering at their progress. "Excellent work." She stood and made her way to each wheel, offering tips and suggestions on how they could improve. She demonstrated the correct way to extend the clay upwards and out without having it collapse, the way to create the soft ripples that ran up and down her vase, and how to make sure it was even on all sides.

By the end of the night, they each had a completed piece to add to the kiln, ready to collect the next day.

"Thank you so much for a wonderful evening, Angelique. That was the most fun I've had in a while," Melissa gushed.

"Looks like your skills are lacking, Jane." Lucious shook his head. "You talk a big talk…"

Melissa laughed. "That's not what I meant!"

Jane looped her arm through Melissa's. "I can assure you, my skills are more than adequate." She leant over, nuzzling her nose below Melissa's ear, making her shiver and her cheeks flush.

She swallowed, her voice husky. "*More* than adequate," she agreed.

Lucious held his palm up. "Nope, that's a little more information than I needed. Unless, of course, you'd like to hear about how wonderful our love life is too?"

"I think we're good," Jane said, elbowing him in the ribs. "But thanks for the offer."

"Ah, I don't think Angelique wants to be hearing about *either* of our sex lives." Raoul tilted his head in her direction with an apologetic smile.

She waved a dismissive hand through the air. "Nothing I haven't seen or heard before. Love is something to be shared and admired not shackled away for no one to see." She gathered her things together, waiting silently by the table.

"Right, well I suppose we'll leave you to your evening then." Lucious took her hands in his. "It was an absolute pleasure watching you work. The kids are going to love it tomorrow."

"Actually," Melissa piped up. "Would it be okay for me to pop back in the morning and take a few pics for the gazette? I'd love to do a feature on what you're doing here, Lucious, and, if it's alright with you, Angelique, perhaps I could interview you and the kids after the class?"

Lucious beamed, swinging Angelique's hands. "What do you think? You up for a bit of free publicity?"

Chapter 14

The argument

"I think that went really well, don't you?" Melissa asked as she pushed the door closed. "It felt good to be creative for a change."

"Ah, you're a journalist. You write for a living. Isn't that creative?" Jane scoffed, tossing her jacket on the couch.

"Hardly. Papers aren't known for their fluffy stories. It's factual and to the point."

"Huh, I never really thought of it that way, but I suppose you're right." She followed Melissa through to the kitchen, where she was pulling mugs down for coffee.

Gravel crunched outside as a car pulled up the drive. "You expecting someone?" Jane asked, moving to the window to peek out.

"No, no one."

"Oh no." Jane grimaced as she let the curtain go moments before the front door opened then slammed, and Vaughn stomped down the hall to their room, not even stopping to say hello.

Melissa frowned, and Jane placed a sympathetic hand on her shoulder. "I'll go make sure they're okay. You deal with him." She nodded towards the door before heading down the hall after Vaughn.

Melissa swung the door open to find Joe on the doorstep, his face set in a scowl and his hand poised, ready to knock.

"What is this nonsense you've been spouting to my daughter?"

"Good to see you too, Joe." She stepped outside, pulling the door closed behind her. "And they're *our* daughter. And I haven't been spouting anything. Care to elaborate?" She folded her arms across her chest, her hip jutted out. It didn't take a rocket scientist to know why he was returning Vaughn mere hours after they'd left, but she wasn't about to make it easy on him. Judging by the way Vaughn rushed through the house, he hadn't made it easy on them either.

"You and this, this, *woman* you're shacking up with." He spat the words with disdain, reminding Melissa once again just how closed minded he could be. "You're filling her mind with nonsense."

"The thing about divorce, *Joe,* is that you don't have any say in who I spend my time with."

"I have a say in who my daughter spends her time with."

"*Our* daughter, and *they* can spend *their* time however they want."

"*She* is a not a group of people! *She* is one person. A girl. And her name is Siobhan."

Melissa stepped in close, all five foot two of her, and looked up at him with hatred in her eyes. "Pull your head out of your arse and join the twenty-first century! Everything isn't just black and white anymore. There are multiple colours in the rainbow, and people don't

86

have to hide who they are anymore." She pointed a finger behind her, in the direction of Vaughn's room. "You should be proud of the fact they know who they are and feel comfortable being that person. It won't have been easy for them to tell you, but they did it because it's important to them, which means it should be important to you too. It's not for you to choose who they can be."

"You think I should be proud my daughter is so confused she doesn't know who she is?"

"For Christ's sake, Joe! They know exactly who they are. That's the point."

"It's preposterous. I refuse to call my daughter by anything other than what she was named at birth. You and that woman are putting ideas in her head, turning her into a freak, and I will not stand for it."

"It's a good thing it's not up to you then, isn't it?"

His eyes narrowed. "She carries *my* last name. That means something."

"Yeah, it means you're their father, but that's where it ends. You can't control them and turn them into a carbon copy of you."

"Don't be ridiculous. She can't be a carbon copy of me, but I will have a say in what she does with her life."

"What they do with their life is irrelevant. We're talking about how you treat them. You can't just stick your head in the sand and pretend things haven't changed. This is who they are, and what they want isn't that difficult to understand."

"She doesn't know what she wants. It's our job to guide her, and you're letting her run around with these ridiculous notions of being something other than what she is."

"I'm doing no such thing. I'm letting them pave their own way."

Joe snorted. "And that's another thing. This 'paving her own way' rubbish has only encouraged her to pursue art instead of business like we'd discussed. Art is a hobby, not a way to make a living. I'd appreciate if you didn't insist on encouraging her."

"I will encourage them to do whatever their heart desires. *That's* what being a good parent is."

"Oh is it? Letting them fail is being a good parent now?" He shook his head. "You seem to be forgetting it's me who will be paying for her studies. I think that gives me a say in the matter."

Melissa's brows shot up, and it took every ounce of energy she had not to ball her fists and deck him one, because that's what he deserved right now. "You can't just throw your money around and think that means you get to decide Vaughn's future. In case you hadn't noticed, they're not interested in business school. Not even remotely. You'd have to be blind to see their passion lies anywhere other than the arts."

"Art school will get her nowhere in life but on the poverty chain. Do you want that for her?"

"Of course I don't, but that's not the reality for everyone, and they have real talent."

Joe scoffed. "Talent means nothing if you've got no smarts to back them up. She's going to business school, and she can cut out this rubbish about being an it or them or whatever it is. I will not stand for it."

Melissa gritted her teeth. "For the last time, *Joe,* it's not your decision if Vaughn goes by he, she, it, or them. If they wanted to go by the name Smokey the Bear, I'd accept that too. It's part of being a parent. You tell me to cut the cords, well maybe you should take a leaf out of your own book. Stop trying to control them."

"I'm not controlling her, I'm ensuring she has a better life than one of a pauper."

Melissa snorted. "Don't pretend this is about anything other than you getting your way." She shook her head. "If art school is what they want, then that's where they're going. And if I have to, I'll find the money for their tuition myself."

His eyes narrowed. "That's not how this works. You know as well as I do your pitiful wage isn't enough to put her through community college, let alone university."

"So I'll get a second job, or they can get a scholarship. Whatever. I'll figure something out. We don't need your money."

"Says the woman who only a few hours ago asked me to pitch in for a suit. If you can't afford a suit for a formal, you sure as hell can't afford tuition," he spat.

"I'll find a way," she ground out through her teeth. "Your money and name might get you what you want out there, but it won't get you anywhere with

Vaughn. They're not like you, and you need to understand that."

He shook his head. "You know, I thought I was doing the right thing by walking away and letting you take the lead over her parenting. I've tried to reason with you, but you've made it quite clear, you're no longer fit to be her mother." He turned on his heels and stalked towards his car. "You'll be hearing from my lawyer."

Melissa's eyes widened, and she stumbled backwards. "W-what?" she stuttered. He was the one who left because 'being a parent wasn't what he'd signed up for' and now he was threatening to take them away? "Joe, you don't mean that."

"I do. I may not be the best father in the world, but I know what is right. Siobhan needs stability and a firm hand. Things you clearly cannot provide for her anymore."

"You're being unreasonable."

He swung around, pointing a finger at her chest. "No, *you're* the unreasonable one. You're just going to let her throw her life away, and I will not accept that. I've let you have your way with her all these years, but I cannot abide this absurdity."

Tears of anger and betrayal stung her eyes, and Melissa swiped them away with the back of her hand. "Have you even bothered to ask them what it is they want? Have you even had a conversation about it? Or have you just told them what you expect and that's that?" She stepped around his pointed finger and into his personal space. "I won't let you treat them the same way you treated me just because you think your name has so much sway. Well, it may have gotten me places I wanted for a time there, but everything I have today is off my own back. Your name had nothing to do with it. And Vaughn doesn't need it either. In fact, they're better off without it if it means you holding them back from who they are."

"She's fifteen! She doesn't know who she is!"

"They know they prefer Vaughn to Siobhan. They know they prefer to wear pants over dresses. They know they don't see themselves as any one gender. In fact, I'd go so far as to say they know themselves a damn sight better than most adults I know. *You* just don't want to see it because it doesn't fit into your perfect little world," she spat. "If you actually bothered to talk to them and listen to what they have to say, maybe you'd see it too." She took a step backwards, watching him wrench the door open and slide in behind the steering wheel, the conversation clearly over.

He slammed the door and started the ignition, barely waiting for it to finish turning over before tearing up the gravel on his way down the drive.

Melissa stood with her arms wrapped around her middle as if she could somehow stop herself from falling apart. A war had started, one she wasn't sure she could win. Joe's name may not have got her where she is today, but she wasn't naïve enough to believe she stood a chance against the lawyers he could afford. Joe didn't like to lose, and he would throw everything in his arsenal at her, just to prove a point. But she wasn't about to give up without a fight. Not when Vaughn's happiness was at stake.

Chapter 15

The morning after the night before

Melissa sat at the kitchen counter, cradling a mug of coffee as if her life depended on it. Vaughn had shut themselves in their room most of the night, only coming out for snacks and bathroom breaks. No amount of coaxing could change it. Melissa hadn't the heart to tell them what had happened with Joe, or how dire the situation was about to get. There was no way she would let him take them away from her. No way.

The soft sound of padding feet on the carpet down the hall caught her attention, and she looked up with a weary smile that didn't reach her eyes. Jane squeezed her shoulders as she went past. "You didn't sleep well either then?"

"I don't think I slept at all. I just kept going over it in my mind, trying to work out where I went wrong. What I could've said to make it right."

Jane huffed out a breath, a frown marring her face. "You didn't do anything wrong. It's all on him."

"But I pushed him too far, and now he's…" Her voice cracked. "He's going to take Vaughn from me."

"That'll never happen. No court of law is going to take a child from a loving parent for letting them be who they are. Not in this day and age."

"He's got money to throw at this though. I don't. He can probably pay people to make shit up about me." She slumped, her face resting on her hand.

"Do you really think he'd do that?"

"I don't know. Maybe. He likes to get his own way."

"But would he slander your name to get it?"

"I honestly don't know anymore. I never thought he'd try and take Vaughn from me."

Jane pressed her lips together. "I've seen you with Vaughn. You're a great mum. To say you're not is low." She rounded the counter, taking Melissa's shoulders in hand and spinning her to face her. There were dark shadows beneath her tear-filled eyes. Jane trailed the pads of her fingertips from Melissa's forehead, down her jaw, and around the base of her throat, linking them behind her neck. "Come here."

Melissa collapsed into her arms, clinging to her as if her life depended on it. "What am I going to do?"

"You're going to get yourself ready for Helping Hands this morning, and then you're going to forget about it for a while and spend some time with Vaughn. Nothing can be done over the weekend."

She was right. Melissa knew this, but it felt wrong to sit back and wait for Joe to fire the first shot when she had no bulletproof vest to protect herself.

"Why don't you go and get into the shower, and I'll whip up some breakfast?"

Melissa stretched her neck backwards, giving Jane a sceptical look. "*You're* going to cook?"

Jane tapped her playfully on the arm. "I can cook."

"Really? Because I've yet to see you so much as lift a spatula."

"That's the long pointy thing, right?"

Melissa snorted, shaking her head. It was impossible to tell if she was serious or not. "Just don't burn the house down, okay?"

"I can't make any promises." Jane dragged her up from the seat and shoved her towards the door. "Now shoo. I've got this."

Slipping quietly down the hall, Melissa stopped outside Vaughn's door. She leaned her head against the wood, pressing her palms flat either side of her. The very idea of Vaughn being taken was too much to bear. She was the one who'd carried them for nine months. The one who'd taught them how to talk and toilet themselves, how to dress and tie their shoes. It had been her who'd waved them off at their first day of school and every day since. It wasn't fair that Joe thought he had any right to tear them apart.

With a deep breath, she eased the door open, peeking inside. Vaughn lay on their side with the blankets pulled up tight around their neck. Tucked in between their arms was an old favourite. The tatty pink bear given to them the day they were born. It had been a while since teddy had made its way beneath the sheets, but it was good to see it still offered some comfort.

"It's creepy to stare, Mum." Vaughn squinted one eye open.

"Sorry, I didn't mean to wake you."

Vaughn sighed rolling onto their back. "You didn't."

Melissa pushed the door open wider, tiptoeing around the clothes on the floor to Vaughn's bed. Under normal circumstances, she'd say something about the untidiness, but now was not the time. "Your father will come around eventually. You have to remember, he's from an older generation. He's set in his ways."

Vaughn rolled their eyes. "You don't have to pretend. He's never going to see me the way you do."

"I think he just needs a little time to adjust to it all."

"I know you don't believe that. I heard you guys talking."

Melissa sucked a breath in through her teeth. "You did, huh?"

"I know you think because you're small, your voice doesn't carry, but it does. Loud and clear. I hear more than you think."

"Oh." Melissa grimaced. "So, you heard…"

Vaughn's brow crinkled, their voice quiet. "Enough to know you're worried and lawyers are getting involved." Tears formed in their eyes, and they swiped a hand across with a sniff. "I can't live with him, Mum. I'll run away before that happens."

"Vaughn," Melissa choked out as she perched on the bed, pulling her daughter into her lap like times of old. "Believe me, I don't want that either, and I'll do everything in my power to keep you here with me."

"But you think he'll win."

Melissa swallowed back the lump in her throat. She had to be more careful what she said and where. "He wants what's best for you, and right now, he doesn't think that's me. So yes, I think he'll do all that he can to prove that." She shifted in her seat, tucking two fingers beneath Vaughn's chin and raising her face to meet her gaze. "But that doesn't mean he'll win. You're older now, and they have to take into account how you feel as well." At least she hoped they did. It had to count for something. "Listen, I'm going down to Helping Hands this morning to interview Lucious and Angelique for the gazette. Why don't you come with me? It'll be good to take your mind off things for a while. They're doing a pottery class."

"I don't know…"

"You can take your frustrations out on the clay," she added in a sing-song voice.

A hint of a smile formed on Vaughn's lips before they nodded. "Okay. But only because I'm tired of being stuck in my room and squeezing the life out of some clay sounds kinda fun." They met their mother's eyes, shrugging their shoulders half-heartedly. Melissa didn't care. If it meant Vaughn would come out of their shell, she'd take it.

"Why don't you ring Mackenzie and see if she wants to join us? She can stay for a sleepover. What do you say?"

Vaughn hesitated, their lips twisted to the side.

"Come on, it'll be fun." Melissa jostled them playfully. "You can see what I made last night. I think you'll be suitably impressed by my efforts." She wiggled her upper body side-to-side, brushing a hand across her shoulder. "Some of my best work."

Vaughn rolled her eyes. "Isn't it the *only* thing you've made with clay before?"

Melissa waved a dismissive hand through the air. "Semantics." She pushed up off the bed with a little more pep in her step now that Vaughn was communicating again. "I'm going to have a shower. Call Mackenzie. We'll swing by her place in half an hour or so." She stopped at the door, returning her gaze to Vaughn. "We'll get through this, honey. I promise."

Chapter 16

The feature

Mackenzie's bubbly exuberance was rather contagious, and within minutes, Vaughn had let go of her sullenness and was sporting a smile, though it didn't quite reach their eyes. When they entered Helping Hands, there were only a few spots left at the tables, and they quickly joined in, while Melissa sought Lucious out.

"Good morning, gorgeous," he whispered, his arms folded across his broad chest. "Angelique removed our creations from the oven this morning. They're over there if you want to have a peek." He pointed to a bench to the side of the room. "Apparently we just need to add some glaze and then she'll whip them back with this lot this afternoon, and we'll have them back on Monday."

"Oh wow, that was quick." She tiptoed across the room, careful not to disturb the class already in session. Right in front of the bench was the beautiful vase Angelique had created, and dotted around behind were the bowl, mug, pen holder, and vase they had created the previous night. Melissa fingered the pen holder, a small smile on her lips. It was going to look great on her desk at work. And it would look right at home with the mug Vaughn had made her.

Loud chatter filled the room as the youths began to squish the clay between their fingers. There were giggles and squelches, and the occasional squeal as someone tried to wipe the muck from their hands onto others. And all the while, Angelique stood up front with a saccharine smile on her face, as if she too understood the joy they were feeling.

There weren't enough wheels to go around, so she split the group into two and had one half work on sculpting by hand while the others tried to spin their creations. If they wanted a go at both, she was happy to stay on longer, which Lucious gave his nod of approval to.

Melissa snapped off a few shots of Angelique with the children, the clay creations they'd made, and a few of the wheels in motion. When she was satisfied she had enough, she made her way back to Lucious, nodding to one of the rooms off to the side. "Shall we go in there?"

He nodded, placing his hand to the small of her back as he guided her across the room.

"Wow, it gets loud in there, huh?"

Lucious grinned. "I have a secret." He pulled two bright orange foam earplugs from his ears. "Don't tell them." He held a finger to his lips.

"Your secret is safe with me." She chuckled. Pulling her phone from her pocket, she brought up the voice recorder. "Do you mind if I record this?"

Lucious waved his hand. "Sure, whatever you need." He took a seat on one of the couches, crossing his ankle over his knee. "Where shall we start?"

"Well, I'd really like to know how you came up with the idea, where all the funds come from, and what plans you have for the future." She sat the phone on the coffee table between them, getting cosy on her own couch. She unravelled her scarf and set it beside her. "Is this something you've always wanted to do?"

Lucious clasped his hands on his lap. "To be honest, no, it wasn't. As you know, my father is the mayor and wanted me to follow in his footsteps, and for a while there, I did consider the idea, but it wasn't really calling to me. It didn't feel like the right move for me. It wasn't until I started hanging out with the Sweetwater Youth while they were getting ready for their performance earlier in the year that the idea came to me. Raoul had been trying to come up with fun activities to do with the children, and I realised there was a need for structured learning, where the youth can come along and gain new skills, at no cost to them. I struggled as a youngster to know what I wanted to do with my life, and I think, had I had the opportunity to try a few things out, it may have made that choice a little easier, and a lot less daunting." He sat forward. "It's a lot of pressure on a fifteen-year-old to decide what their future is going to be so they can do all the right courses, you know?"

"Mmm, it is. I know I would've liked to have had a bit of insight into what was involved before going ahead with my studies."

"Exactly. University or polytechnic courses can be expensive, and if you don't know what you want to do, then you can end up racking up a lot of debt." He gestured to the other room, which was becoming increasingly louder. "And they get to have a bit of fun too. Who doesn't want to learn how to sculpt things out of clay or how to shoot a crossbow?"

"Not so much the crossbow, though that might come in handy with my ex-husband." She rolled her eyes. "But the sculpting was a blast." She grinned, sitting forward. "And what sort of classes do you have planned for the future? Obviously we have sculpting happening right now, but what else do you have lined up?"

His eyes lit up. "Anything you can think of. Next week, I have a budgeting advisor coming to show them how to budget within their means and how to balance their accounts. I've organised someone to help with tax returns, an Olympic shooter coming to show techniques for shooting with a rifle and crossbow, an author and illustrator to discuss the ins and outs of publishing. And a lot more are in the works too. We're just ironing out a few kinks, but we'd like to offer some of these classes to our adult community too, at a subsidised rate, of course. So there's a lot going on in the background."

"That sounds fabulous, and, if you don't mind me saying, a little too good to be true. Who is fronting the bill for all of this?"

"I put up a lot of my own to get Helping Hands off the ground. I bought this building, and with the help of a few mates, we had a little working bee to splash a bit of paint on the walls and set it up with tables and chairs. I purchased a few of those pottery wheels through there to get this class up and running.

Angelique supplied the others from her studio, so they'll be going back with her. The Creative Co-op group has grants available, which I'm applying for too."

"Sounds as if you've thought of everything."

Lucious chuckled. "I don't know about that, but I've definitely put a lot of thought into it, and I'm always open to ideas."

"And if any of our readers have skills they'd like to offer up, are they able to reach out to you?"

"Absolutely. The more classes I can offer, the better. It's about building the community up and helping those who are in need. If you have a skill, chances are, someone out there would like to learn it, so any offers of help are much appreciated. My door is always open."

"Wonderful." Melissa leant forward, retrieving her phone and switching the recorder off. "I think that about covers it. I'd just like to grab a few pictures of you out front, if that's okay, and perhaps some of you mixing with the kids?"

"Sure, whatever you need." He uncrossed his leg, sitting forward. "I'm at your disposal."

Melissa laughed. "Don't say that, I might take advantage." She screwed her eyes closed, shaking her head. "I didn't mean that the way it sounded."

He held his hands out. "That's what this place is all about, Mel. If you need something, don't be afraid to ask."

"No… it's not… I doubt there's anything you could do to help with what I need." She offered a weak smile. "But thank you."

Lucious frowned. "Does this have anything to do with the ex you'd like to use a crossbow on?"

"That obvious, huh? What gave it away?"

"Just a hunch."

She huffed, leaning her head on the back of the couch and throwing her hand across her face. "It's all so complicated, and just an outright mess." Tears welled in her eyes, and she had to fight to keep them from trailing down her cheeks.

"I know we don't know each other all that well, but I *do* know Jane, and you're important to her, so whatever it is, if I can help, I will. Come on, I'm a pretty good listener." He reached across the table, patting his hand on her knee. "What's going on?"

She filled him in on everything, from Vaughn's gender identity to Joe's response and the impending lawsuit. Lucious listened with a thoughtful expression, which quickly morphed into one of anger on her behalf. When Melissa finished, she dropped her head into her hands, letting out a long, drawn-out breath. "I told Vaughn I'd do what I could to stop him taking them, but honestly—" she raised her tormented gaze to his, "—I don't know if I can fight him. A good lawyer is out of my budget, and I doubt legal aid will be able to offer me the same sort of defence."

"You *are* having a rough time, aren't you? But you know what? You've come to the right place. I think I may be able to help with your lawyer issue."

"Oh no." Melissa shook her head. "I wasn't meaning… I couldn't ask you to do that. You've got enough on your plate with this place."

Lucious smiled, stretching his long legs out in front of him. "Things are under control here, so it's no bother. And I happen to know someone I went to school with who might be interested in some pro bono work." He splayed his hands out in front of him. "I can't promise anything, but leave it with me. I'll give them a call and see what we can do."

Chapter 17

The pizza party

The sweet sound of laughter echoed down the hall, making Melissa breathe a sigh of relief. Mackenzie and Vaughn had spent much of the afternoon playing Pictionary, which was Vaughn's forte, and now they were onto Just Dance, which was where Mackenzie's strengths were. Vaughn, unfortunately, had been born with two left feet like their mother. Aside from the old two step, dancing did not come naturally to either of them, hence the hysterics. No matter how hard they tried, Vaughn's hips did not twist and bend like their friend's.

"I told you they'd be fine." Jane nudged a glass of wine across the counter. "Which means you can put your feet up and stop worrying for the night. I'll take care of dinner."

Melissa took a sip of her wine, giving Jane a look of incredulity. "Uh, it's not that I don't appreciate the offer, but maybe we should leave the cooking to me." After her shower that morning, she'd come out to find Jane standing at the counter with a piece of burnt toast in one hand and a bowl of stodgy porridge in the other. Needless to say, she'd started her day with little more than a strong cup of coffee.

Jane snorted. "I said I'd take care of it, not that I'd cook it." She waved her phone in the air. "Pizza?"

Melissa huffed out a laugh. "Pizza sounds perfect." And much more appetising than porridge.

While Jane placed the order, Melissa made her way through to the lounge, curling up on the couch with her glass of wine in hand. The day hadn't been nearly as bad as she'd expected. After the interview with Lucious and Angelique and a few more snaps taken, she'd added a layer of green glaze to her pen holder, ready for another go in the oven. The whole activity had been therapeutic, and she was considering joining the adult classes Lucious had mentioned. Perhaps it was something she and Vaughn could do together.

"All done." Jane padded into the room, placing her wine on the coffee table. She rounded the back of the couch and took hold of Melissa's shoulders, her fingers gently kneading the knots.

"Mmm, that feels good." Melissa rolled her head forward, letting the stress of the past few days wash away with every caress. "You're good at that."

"See? Who needs to be able to cook when you have the touch of an angel?" She spread her fingers out on either side of Melissa's face, waggling them.

"I suppose you're right. We all have our uses. Yours just isn't in the kitchen."

"Which is why we make a great team, don't you think?" She curled her upper body around so her face was in line with Melissa's. Her hands slid down to wrap her in a bear hug from behind.

Melissa smiled, nuzzling her nose with Jane's. "I do." She arched her chin upwards, her lips brushing gently across Jane's.

"Oh, sorry." Mackenzie covered her eyes, backing out of the room. "I didn't see anything, I swear."

Jane chuckled, straightening up. "You can relax. No more acts of PDA, I promise." She skirted around the couch, sitting next to Melissa. "Hope you're hungry. Pizza should be here in a few minutes."

Mackenzie pulled her hands from her face, her eyes still squinched together as if she didn't fully believe there was no funny business going on. When she was satisfied it was safe, her shoulders sagged with relief and she grinned. "Awesome, thanks. I was just coming out to see if we could grab a snack or something."

Melissa frowned. "I hope Vaughn didn't send you out here to ask in their place."

"I don't mind." Mackenzie shrugged.

Melissa leaned forward, nodding her head down the hall. "How're they doing?"

"Umm, as good as can be expected, I guess." She gave another half shrug. "All they really want is for him to accept it and try, you know? It's not like they'll get angry or upset if you muck it up." She twisted her lips to the side. "It took me a few days to get used to it, and I still sometimes forget, but Vaughn's cool about it, you know?"

Melissa nodded, though a part of her wondered how long Vaughn had been keeping this from her.

Teenage daughters are notorious for keeping secrets from their parents, but she'd always prided herself in their closeness and in providing what she thought was a safe space. She only wished Vaughn had felt they could come to her sooner. "I know. We just have to keep on trying and hope he comes to his senses before he pushes them away completely."

Mackenzie pulled her lips into a thin line, ducking her head. "I think it's already too late. They're pretty cut up about it." She glanced behind her before stepping into the room quickly. "You can't make them go back there." Her eyes were wide and imploring. "Please. I think they might run away or... something."

Melissa's pulse quickened. "What do you mean 'or something'? Mackenzie, has Vaughn said something to you?" She scooted forward in her seat, her elbows landing on her knees. She swallowed thickly. "Has she... *they*... Have they said they'll hurt themselves?" Her voice was barely more than a whisper.

"No, but..." Mackenzie glanced behind her again, as if she was sure Vaughn was about to jump out at any moment.

"But you think they might?"

She toyed with her fingers, twisting them together. "I don't know. Maybe." Tears filled her eyes, and she sniffed. "I'm just worried... My uncle..." She let her voice trail off, and Melissa recalled Vaughn telling her how Mackenzie hadn't been at school for a few weeks because her uncle had taken his own life.

There'd been no warning. No signs. Of course she was worried.

"Oh, honey, we all are." Melissa jumped to her feet, rushing over and pulling Mackenzie into her arms. "It's a difficult time for everyone right now, but we'll get through this together, okay?" She pulled back, taking hold of Mackenzie's shoulders. "You're a really good friend, which is what they need right now. You have no idea how much of a difference you've made just by being here today."

Mackenzie nodded, lowering her head.

"I mean it. Vaughn is lucky to have you."

"Thanks, Miss Hobart. I'm lucky to have them too."

"Just promise me you'll let me know if you think they're in any danger, okay? Let me know so I can do something before it's too late. They need us all on their side right now."

"I will. I promise." She wiped her eyes and flapped her hands in front of her face. "Do I look like I've been crying?" Her bottom lip quivered.

Melissa's palm smoothed down her arm. "You look fine."

The doorbell chimed, and Jane jumped up. "That'll be the pizza." As she brushed past, she rubbed her hand on Mackenzie's shoulder in solidarity. "A good friend is like a good bra. They offer support and hold you up when you can no longer hold yourself up. The world needs more good bras, and you, my friend, are a good bra."

Mackenzie snort-laughed. "Uh, thanks?"

Jane nodded, carrying on through to the entry.

"Don't mind her. She compared me to granny panties the other day."

When Mackenzie laughed and asked her why, she simply said, "Because I'm reliable and cover all the important bits." She shrugged. "It's kind of my job, so she's not wrong."

"Pizza!" Jane called as she kicked the door closed. "Come and get it while it's hot." She slid four pizza boxes onto the counter.

"How many people are you feeding?" Melissa asked with a quirked brow.

"What? Not enough?"

With a laugh, Melissa opened one of the boxes, peering inside. "Four is plenty. Unless they're all seafood." She turned her nose up. "Gross."

"But you ate salmon at the restaurant," Jane pointed out, grabbing a slice and taking a bite. She slid the box off the top and pushed the rest towards Melissa.

"Salmon is different. It actually has flavour that isn't just sea water. And don't get me started on the textures." The next box was Hawaiian. "This is more like it."

"And you think *shrimp* have a funny texture?" Jane screwed her nose up. "Pineapple is stringy and gets stuck in your teeth. It also doesn't belong on pizza, but I knew the kids would like it." She looked Melissa up and down. "I thought you'd have better taste."

"Don't knock it until you've tried it. Next you'll be telling me you can't put spaghetti on pizza." She snorted, and Jane looked aghast.

"I don't even know who you are right now."

"What? You never tried it?"

"Uh, no, why would I?"

"It used to be a delicacy when I was growing up. You'd start with a scone-like base, that you'd roll flat, top it with a can of spaghetti, ham, and grated cheese. It was delicious." Melissa inhaled deeply, closing her eyes at the memory.

"That. Sounds. Disgusting." Jane swallowed her mouthful as if it was a wadge of dirt. "And wrong on so many levels."

"I hate to break it to you, Mum, but it's not as appealing as you think it is." Vaugh slunk in, grabbing a piece of Hawaiian from the box and shovelling it into her mouth. "I mean, it was fun to make," she said around her mouthful, "but you can't beat a Sliceroni pizza."

Melissa shook her head in mock sadness. She let out a sigh. "All these years, I thought you liked our homemade pizza parties."

"I liked the party part, and the making them part. Just not so much the eating part." Vaughn grimaced. "Sorry."

Melissa laughed, rubbing her forehead with a greasy hand. "I can't believe you let me feed you something you hated every Saturday of your primary school years."

Vaughn shrugged. "You were always so happy when we were making them."

Unbidden, tears sprung to Melissa's eyes. "You really are the best, you know that?" She flung her arm around Vaughn, pulling them in for a lopsided hug.

"It's just pizza, Mum." They rolled their eyes, but their arm found its way around Melissa's waist, squeezing tight.

Mackenzie leaned in, whispering loudly behind her hand. "My mum gets weird about food too."

Jane mouthed 'hormones' over Melissa's shoulder, and the two friends giggled.

"You'll understand when you have your own children," Melissa said. "I guarantee you'll find yourself a ball of tears too." She pointed at her chest. "I wasn't always this way."

"She used to cry when she came to the school assemblies and watched other children get awards." Vaughn smirked.

"I was just so proud for them!" Melissa clutched a hand to her chest. "They were so small and adorable, and it made my heart swell to see them look so happy."

Vaughn rolled her eyes. "Yeah, but you didn't even know any of them."

"I don't have to know them to feel pride."

"It's a mum thing," Jane offered. "Don't worry, you won't catch me blubbering over your awards. I'll leave the waterworks to this one." She hooked her thumb at Melissa, who smiled knowingly.

"Just you wait. Your time will come."

Chapter 18

The helping hand

The photos from Helping Hands came out nicely, and Melissa had the difficult task of choosing which ones to use, both on the cover of the gazette and with the feature she'd written. Lucious was getting a two-page spread, including a list of the upcoming classes available, and a shout out to Angelique and her studio. With any luck, it would benefit them both, and Angelique would be back more frequently.

As it was, she was returning that evening with the finished products from Friday and Saturday's classes, and Melissa couldn't wait to hold her creation in her hand and put it to use on her desk. She was dying to see what Vaughn had made too. Angelique had packed it away before she'd had a chance.

The heavy wooden door scraped across the floor as Lucious entered with a tall, broad-shouldered woman in tow. His eyes swept the room before landing on Melissa, and he gave her a wave as he swaggered towards her.

"Melissa, I hope you don't mind me stopping in at work, but I have someone for you to meet." He gestured towards his companion. "This is Robyn Hargreaves, the lawyer I told you about."

Robyn nodded, holding her hand out. Melissa accepted the offer, her small hand engulfed by Robyn's. "Pleased to meet you."

"Likewise, though it's unfortunate it's under such circumstances." Robyn pressed her lips into a thin line. "I understand you're having trouble with your ex-husband threatening a lawsuit?"

"I am, yes." Melissa cleared her throat, looking uncomfortable. "I appreciate you coming to meet with me." She glanced at Lucious. "But I'm sorry, I don't think I can afford you. I don't want to waste your time."

Robyn smiled, taking Melissa's hand in hers. "Lucious already explained the situation, and I'm happy to do this one pro bono. These contentious cases are my specialty."

Tears welled in Melissa's eyes. "Really? Are you sure?"

"I am."

"You have no idea what this means to me. Thank you." She stifled her sob, swiping a finger beneath her eyes to stop her mascara from running.

"It's my pleasure." Robyn gestured towards Melissa's desk. "I can see you're busy, so I won't keep you much longer, but if we could get together in the next day or so to go over the details, that would be great. I'm in town until Wednesday."

"Oh, you're not from here?" Melissa frowned. "Do you have far to travel?" She hated to inconvenience anyone, especially when they were going out of their way to help her.

"No, not far. I'm based in Brookhaven, so I travel for most cases." She pulled her phone from her pocket and tapped the screen. "In fact, how are you placed this evening? The sooner we can get started on this, the sooner I can work my magic."

"This evening is perfect. I just have to swing by Helping Hands to pick some things up, then I'm all yours."

"Great. In the meantime, I need you to think about whether there is anything from your past or present that may be dragged up. Anything that could be twisted against you. It's much easier to have a strategy in place than have to work something out on the fly."

"Oh, um, okay."

"Family court is not like what you see on the TV. It's much more intimate, but that doesn't mean it can't get messy."

"Right, well, nothing comes to mind."

"That's great. Children are usually kept out of the courtroom for these cases, but because of Vaughn's age, they'll most likely be asked to state their case too. They need to be prepared for that."

"Right." Vaughn had never been one to back down from speaking out, so that shouldn't be a problem.

"And I'll need you to think about some character references too. People who know you as a person and a mother. They need to be willing to speak on the day, but if you can get written references, that's a start."

Melissa nodded, jotting it down.

"Shall we say seven o'clock this evening?"

117

"Yes, great."

"Seeing as you're already heading in to Helping Hands this evening, why don't you use it for headquarters?" Lucious offered, pulling a key from his pocket and handing it to Melissa. "You'd be doing me a favour by being there to let Angelique in with her boxes of pottery for everyone to collect." He smiled, giving her a wink. "Then I can surprise Raoul with a nice dinner out."

"If you're sure?"

"Of course. Mi casa, su casa. And, before you ask, I'd be honoured to be a character reference for you."

"Oh gosh. I don't know what to say." More tears threatened to fall, and this time, she let them. Being a solo mother for almost half her life had made her fiercely independent and reluctant to rely on others, but for the first time in a long time, she was glad to have others in her corner. She was glad to not have to go through this alone. "Thank you."

"Of course. That's what friends are for, right?" Lucious reached out, letting his hand fall to her forearm. "I think you'll find a lot of people will be happy to help out. You're our number one journalist. You're like an integral part of the community, and no one is going to want to see you or Vaughn fall."

Sniffing, Melissa brushed her tears away. Her bottom lip quivered as she nodded. "That means a lot, thank you."

"Right then. We'll leave you to it, and I'll see you this evening." Robyn proffered her hand once more. "It was lovely to meet you."

"Likewise. I can't thank you enough for taking this on."

"Your daughter has a right to be listened to, and I intend to make sure they're heard. Getting them a fair hearing is all the thanks I need." She turned to Lucious, waving a hand towards the door. "Shall we?"

Melissa slumped into her chair, her eyes finding the framed picture of her and Vaughn taken last Christmas, before life took a chaotic turn. Vaughn had Melissa's face shape and mouth, but their eyes were all Joe. Piercing blue eyes that could turn your blood to ice if you crossed them, but also vibrant and full of life when times were good. They say the eyes are a window to the soul, but Vaughn's have always been a mirror of their emotions. She remembered staring into those crystalline eyes when Vaughn was mere days old, thinking how much they resembled the sea on a calm day, but how quickly they could change, as if storm clouds had rolled on in.

These days it seemed a perpetual cloud hung in their eyes with barely a glimpse of that bright, calmness, and not for the first time, Melissa wondered just how long Vaughn had been hurting. Something told her it had been a long while.

Chapter 19

The L word

The meeting with Robyn went well, and both left feeling as though they had a chance. Lucious had already agreed to be a character reference, and she'd asked Sandra Smith of Smith's Steel Mill to do so too. After her husband Warren had died, Melissa had written up a piece about his life and what he'd done for the community, and Sandra had never forgotten it. They had become quite good friends while she'd been gathering all the details she needed for the feature, and even now, they continued to meet once a month for a coffee and catch up. It was one of the best parts of her job; getting to know the people behind the stories. That had been the driving force behind her career choice. The opportunity to get behind doors and find out what was really going on. To see what made people tick. To uncover the truth.

Robyn had suggested having a few references lined up from people of all walks of life, who could vouch for her both as a mother and professional. It was impossible to know what Joe was going to throw their way, and they wanted to be prepared for the worst.

The problem was, if it wasn't work or child related, she'd kept to herself over the years. Vaughn had been her constant companion, but she could hardly use her own daughter as a reference.

She'd thought about asking Giancarlo, the upstanding man that he was would probably hold some sway, but they'd only known each other a little while, and all fleeting visits. It felt rude to even ask.

Jane had offered, but Melissa was worried it would come across as biased seeing as they were sleeping together. No doubt Joe would have a thing or two to say about it too.

"There must be loads of people you can ask," Jane said as she waved the waitress over. "Think about all the people you've given publicity to over the years, or the other mums you've met at school pick up or camps or whatever."

The waitress sauntered over, chewing gum loudly. "What can I get you?"

"Some manners for a start," Jane said under her breath, raising her brows at Melissa.

The girl's mouth hung open, and Melissa gently reached up, pushing it closed. "I think she just means for you to chew with your mouth closed." She gave her a wink then glanced down at her menu. "I'll have a chai with coconut milk please."

The waitress blinked once, twice, then turned to Melissa with a nod. "Anything else?"

"I'll have the same. And one of those pieces of chocolate fudge in the cabinet." Jane pointed.

"Mmhmm," the girl mumbled, spinning on her heel.

"Wait!" Jane reached out, and the girl's gaze fell to where Jane was now holding onto her hand. "Sorry. I just... I shouldn't have said what I said. Please don't spit in my food." She offered a smile, and the girl's lip curled. Jane reared back, her hand dropping to her side. "Rude."

Melissa chuckled. "You did kind of tell her off."

"And then I apologised."

"Is that what you call it? It seemed more like an afterthought when you realised she's serving you food." Melissa sniggered.

"So it didn't bother you she sounded like a cow chewing cud?" Jane quirked her brow, waiting her out. They'd only known each other a few days before Melissa had admitted her aversion to the sound of people chewing. Something about it really grated her nerves.

"Okay, yes. You know it bothered me." An involuntary shudder ran down her spine. "I just wouldn't have said anything."

"And that's why I'm here." Jane grinned. "To keep your delicate ears from hearing the sound of others masticating."

"I beg your pardon?" an elderly gentleman commented from the table beside them. "That's not very ladylike language."

"I said *masticated,* as in chewing." She made the motion with her mouth. "And I would think listening in on other people's conversations wasn't very gentlemanly either." She gave him a pointed stare.

He rustled his newspaper loudly and turned his back on them, muttering, "Well I never."

A different waitress weaved through the tables holding a tray with two cups and a slice of fudge.

"See? Look. She can't even face you now. She sent someone else." Melissa tilted her head towards the waitress as she came closer.

"Two chai lattes with coconut milk and chocolate fudge?" she asked, placing them on the table before they'd even answered her.

"Thank you," Melissa said to her retreating back. She eyed her drink before pushing it to the centre of the table. "I don't know if I trust these drinks now."

Jane had already cut a chunk of her fudge and taken a bite. She scrunched her nose, tossing the delicacy around in her mouth before swallowing slowly. "I've suddenly lost my appetite." She slid her plate and cup in to join Melissa's.

"I guess they won't be on my list of character references." Melissa rested her chin on her hand, glancing at the two girls who were standing behind the serving hatch giving them the stink eye, as Vaughn would call it.

"No, but they're not really the demographic you want anyway. Too young." She sat in thought for a moment before looking up with excitement. "What about Mackenzie? Maybe she could ask her parents?"

"That's actually not a bad idea. Mackenzie has come on holiday with us before, and she's stayed over multiple times over the years. If anyone is going to know what kind of mother I am, it's her and her parents."

"Exactly." Jane reached across the table, cupping her hand around Melissa's. "We've got this. Anyone with eyes can see how good a mother you are to Vaughn."

"Thanks. Let's just hope the courts see it that way too."

"They will. You're impossible not to love."

Melissa blinked, her cheeks heating. "Um, did you just say you love me?"

Jane picked at the fudge, forming balls of icing between her fingers then flicking them onto the saucer. "Did I?"

"That's what it sounded like."

Jane's eyes drifted up to meet Melissa's. "Then I guess I must've." She wiped her fingers on a napkin, sitting back. "Is that okay?"

Melissa huffed out a breath. "Oh my god, yes." She tugged at her collar, suddenly feeling too warm. "Sorry, you just took me by surprise." She chuckled, reaching across the table to take Jane's sticky hand. "It's more than okay."

Chapter 20

The meeting

Two weeks had flown by since their first meeting, and Melissa was nervous to hear what Robyn had discovered. She'd seemed invigorated on the phone, and Melissa couldn't help but hope it meant good news. Perhaps the end of the lawsuit altogether?

She stepped into the corridor of Helping Hands, closing the door quietly behind her. Lucious poked his head around the corner, ushering her down the hall to his office. "She's in here." He gave her a warm smile, placing a hand to the small of her back as she went past him. "I'll grab some coffees while you two talk."

"Melissa." Robyn stood, brushing a hand down her tailored jacket. She shook Melissa's hand then gestured for her to sit.

Spread on the table in front of her was an open manilla folder with sheafs of paper and photos paperclipped to them.

"Melissa, how much do you know about your ex-husband's earlier years? Before he met you."

Perching on the couch with her hands held rigid on her knees, she pursed her lips. "Only what he told me. He lost his parents in an accident when he was a teenager. He used what little they left him to get through university and worked his way up the ranks."

She cast a glance at the paperwork in front of her. "Is there something I should know?"

"I'm very thorough with my cases. I like to know who I'm dealing with, on both sides. You have been forthcoming with me, which is appreciated, but it seems your ex hasn't been so forthcoming with you."

"I see."

"Are you aware he changed his name some years ago?" She pulled a slip of paper out of the folder, handing it over. "He was born Joseph Keith Solomon. His parents, Darlene and Ken, are both still alive and well." She pulled a photo from the pile and slid it across the table.

"Oh my god." Melissa stared at the grainy image of a man and woman holding a young boy between them. They all had the same crystal blue eyes.

"Lovely people." Robyn paused, meeting Melissa's gaze. "They haven't seen him in thirty years. They had no idea he even had a daughter."

Closing her eyes, Melissa rubbed her temples. She'd expected him to have skeletons, but not of this magnitude.

"When he was sixteen, he took a job with an elderly gentleman by the name of Philip Balderson. He was a banker, and a wealthy one at that. From all accounts, Joe was a driven young man who made himself indispensable. He soaked up all the knowledge Philip had to offer him, and when he took ill, it was Joe who nursed him. When he died, he left a hefty sum to Joe, and that's when he changed his name, finished his schooling, and started up his own corporate banking firm."

Melissa slumped back in her seat, her mind reeling. "I'm sorry, this is a lot to take in."

"I understand. Take your time." Robyn shuffled the papers around, closing the folders and piling them on top of each other.

"So, let me get this straight," she started slowly. "He disowned his family to become something 'more'?" She made air quotes around the word. "His own flesh and blood wasn't good enough so he just pretended they didn't exist?" Anger surged through her veins. "He used someone else's name to further his career. The name he's so quick to point out will get you places." She laughed without humour. "He's been waving this moniker around as if the world owes him respect, when in actual fact, he *stole* the identity and used it as his own. And *he* thinks *he* should be the one making decisions for our daughter?" She shook her head. "That self-righteous arsehole."

"That's one way of putting it."

"Does any of this work in my favour?" There was a bitter taste in her mouth. All these years she'd thought she knew him. "Clearly family doesn't mean as much to him as he's preaching."

"It could prove useful, yes. He's done well to make it this far without anyone finding out. I daresay he will have paid a few people to turn a blind eye to his humble beginnings and possibly nefarious change of circumstances."

Melissa's mouth gaped. "Are you saying...?"

Robyn raised a brow. "Nothing concrete, but it's awfully suspect that the real Mr. Balderson changed his will to include Joe only a month before his death."

"No." She shook her head vehemently. "No, there's no way he had a hand in it. He might be many things, but he's not a murderer."

"No, you're right. He's not a murderer, but he's definitely someone who took advantage of an old man's generosity, and he may not want that to get out. We may be able to use this to settle outside of court, if that's what you want."

It would mean Vaughn wouldn't have to stand in front of strangers while they decide their fate. It would save them both the time and stress, not to mention the many hours Robyn would no doubt have to put in. But then what? Joe gets to go back to his fake life, pretending to be someone he's not? He continues making Vaughn feel less than in his eyes? He never has to face up to his parents and explain why he ostracised them? That hardly seemed fair.

"I don't know. Can I think about it?"

"By all means. This is your case, your decision. In the meantime, I'll continue digging, see what else I can come up with. How did you get on with the references?"

Melissa rifled through her bag, pulling out a clear plastic sleeve. "I have five so far." Mackenzie's parents had been great, both offering to write something, and Raoul had come to the party too. It seemed they had a lot of people willing to go to bat for them.

130

Robyn flicked through them, skim reading each one. "These are good. They'll do nicely." She added them to her pile and stood. "I'll be in town overnight if you need to reach me. You have my number."

"Right. Yes." Melissa stood, brushing her hands down her front. "Thank you for meeting with me, and for all—" she gestured at the files on the table, "—this. It was enlightening, to say the least." She moved towards the door, stopping midway. "Robyn?"

"Mm?"

"What would you do, if you were me?"

"Honestly? If someone threatened to take my kid away from me, I think I'd take them to the cleaners, expose them for who they really are." She folded her arms across her chest. "But I'm vindictive and like to have the last word."

"If it was just me in the crossfire, I think I'd go that route too, but…"

"You want to do right by Vaughn."

"Yeah. They're my number one priority right now."

"Understandable. Maybe talk it out with them. See how they want to proceed. No point winning a case if it means losing what you're fighting for in the first place." Robyn glanced at her watch. "How long does it take to get a coffee? Is he grinding the beans himself?"

Chapter 21

The phone call

"You're joking." Jane's mouth hung agape. "This whole time he's been preaching about Vaughn having to be who they were born as, and he's been lying about his true identity?" She pushed her sleeves up as if readying for a fight. "That arrogant son of a bitch."

"I know. I'm still trying to wrap my head around it. I can't imagine how his parents must feel, knowing he chose to walk away. They didn't even know they were grandparents. Vaughn has missed out on that special bond, and so have they." Melissa shook her head. "It's unfathomable to me that someone could do that to their own family. I thought I knew him."

"Hey." Jane took hold of her hand, bringing her palm to her lips. "You did know him. It just wasn't the whole him, only the him he wanted you to see."

"Yeah, but it still doesn't make me feel any less of a fool. I married him. I had a child with him. I should've asked more questions. I mean, it's part of my profession to dig deep for Christ's sake." She brought her hand up to massage her temples.

"Don't be so hard on yourself. You thought you were in love with the guy. No one thinks straight when they're in love. Hell, I've had some doozies of relationships, and it's only after the fact that I could see how bad they were. We've all been there."

Melissa gave her a look of incredulity. "I doubt very much that everyone has been in a relationship with someone who stole another man's identity, disowned his family, and went on to become a snobbish prick."

"Okay, maybe not *everyone* has had that experience, but I know of several who fell in love with men or women who turned out to be monumental pricks. All I'm saying is, it's not your fault you didn't know. You're a kind and trusting person who expects the same from others, which is a good thing. It's just unfortunate Joe didn't see things the same way." She frowned. "Well, it's unfortunate for you two, but kind of worked in my favour."

Melissa huffed out a laugh, offering a grin. "Sorry, I'm being a Debbie Downer, aren't I?"

Jane held her thumb and forefinger up, merely a millimetre between them. "Little bit." She grinned. "But you're entitled to. It had to be a shock to the system."

"You can say that again."

Jane trailed a finger through the crumbs on her plate. "Are you going to tell Vaughn what you found out?"

"I think I have to, don't I? They have a right to know who their father is." She twisted the teaspoon through the foam in her cup, distorting the cinnamon leaf that had been left there by the talented barista. "I just don't know how to tell her...*them*." She tapped the teaspoon on the side of the cup before laying it on the saucer. "I don't know what the right thing to do is. They never prepared me for any of this at antenatal class or any other parenting class I've been to. I'm flying blind here."

"I wish I had the answer for you." Jane picked her cup up with two hands, taking a sip. "You could try focusing on the positive – that they have another set of grandparents to meet." She shrugged.

"I guess." She took the spoon up again, dipping it into the froth and bringing it to her lips. "What if they're total arseholes?"

Jane snorted out a laugh. "I mean, considering how he turned out, I suppose there's a high probability of that. Or—" she drew the word out, "—and I think this is more likely, they're absolute gems who come from humble beginnings, and that wasn't enough for Joe." With her cup poised at her lips, she tilted her head. "Why don't you give them a call? What's the worst that could happen?" She sipped her latte, licking the foam from her top lip. "If they're complete knobends, then it's no real loss, is it? You don't even need to tell Vaughn about them. But if they're lovely, as Robyn insinuated, then Vaughn gets bonus grandparents, and maybe it's one more set of people on our side when we go to court."

We.

She said when *we* go to court. Melissa's heart leapt into her throat. Of course, she'd hoped Jane would come, but she hadn't wanted to put her on the spot and ask her outright. This woman surprised her every day.

She seemed to know just what Melissa needed, sometimes even before she did herself.

And as per usual, what Jane was saying made sense. She was 100% right. Unlike her, Jane wasn't an overthinker. She saw things as they were and made snap decisions based on what she knew. It was a trait Melissa admired in her. Even as a journalist, she'd always erred on the side of caution, never wanting to rock the boat.

Jane turned her cup on the saucer. "You'll regret it if you don't try. You know you will."

Once again, Jane was right. She *would* regret it if she didn't reach out to them. It was the right thing to do, for them and for Vaughn. They had a right to know who their family was and where they came from, and if that meant Melissa had to bite the bullet and reach out to complete strangers, then so be it.

She pulled her phone from her bag and placed it on the table alongside the card Robyn had given her with their details.

Darlene and Ken Solomon lived on the outskirts of Northpark, a town about two hours' drive from Sweetwater Close. All this time they'd been a short drive's distance away and they'd had no idea.

Jane pushed up from the table. "I'm going to go to the bathroom and then get us another drink, okay?" She nodded towards the phone. "Give you some space."

Melissa smiled gratefully. "Thanks." She watched Jane's hips sway as she walked away before dragging her attention back to the matter at hand. Sucking her lips in between her teeth, she quickly picked up the phone and dialled.

Someone picked up after the first ring. *"Hello?"*

"Uh, hi, is that Darlene Solomon?"

"This is she."

"My name is Melissa Hobart—"

There was a gasp then a muffled sound, as if the phone had been dropped.

"Hello?"

"Sorry, dear. I... you took me by surprise. I was hoping you'd call."

Chapter 22

The confrontation

"What are you doing here?" Melissa demanded, stepping out onto the doorstep and forcing Joe to take a step back. "You can't be here until after the court case." She folded her arms across her chest.

"I thought perhaps you might have come to your senses about fighting this, but I can see that's not the case. You don't know what you're up against. You're making a mistake."

"*I'm* making a mistake? You're the one who started this whole thing."

"Because someone has to look out for our daughter and her future. No one is going to hire someone who doesn't even know their own gender for Christ's sake."

"Vaughn's gender shouldn't have any effect on future job prospects. Not everyone is as closed-minded as you."

He shoved his hands in his pockets, scoffing. "I'm not closed-minded, I'm realistic, which is far from what you're being. First with this non-binary bullshit, and then with your encouraging her to pursue this silly fad of art. You know as well as I do that you can't afford it anyway. You're setting her up to fail."

"If you're so worried about them failing, then step up and come to the party." She flung her arms out wide. "No one is stopping you from helping out."

"I'll give you money right now if you can convince her to give up art and do something academic. It doesn't have to be banking; she could follow in your footsteps for all I care. I can still help her like I did you." He pulled out his cheque book. "Name your price and it's yours, just get her to see sense."

Melissa threw her arms in the air. "They *are* seeing sense! It's you who can't see that. Do you even know that they've been asked to paint a mural at the Sweetwater Youth centre? A whole wall will be covered in their artwork. They don't ask people with no talent to do things like that."

"I'm not saying she isn't any good at it, but it's not going to get her places, is it? How many wealthy artists do you know?"

"Believe it or not, *Joseph Solomon,* not everything is about money and prestige."

He reared back as if he'd been slapped. "Where did you hear that name?"

"I have a good lawyer. She clued me in on a few things you've been keeping from me."

He jutted his chin, like he always did when she said something he didn't like. "So I changed my name. Lots of people do it."

"Yes, they do. But what lots of people don't do, is adopt someone else's name to get them ahead. All this bullshit was about it being *your* name that

Vaughn's besmirching by being a non-binary artist, when in actual fact, it's not even your real name!"

"It may not have been the name I was given at birth, but it's been my name for the past thirty years, and it's gotten me where I am today. And, if you'll cast your mind back, I'm sure you remember how much you liked using my name to get you into places too." He smirked as if he'd won, but as far as Melissa was concerned, he was still missing the point.

"I was twenty when we met! Yes, I'll admit it was a novelty to say your name and have doors open for me, but none of it was real. I'm prouder of what I've accomplished without your name than what I ever accomplished with it."

"You write a free community newspaper. It's hardly worthy of a Pulitzer Prize. Think what you could've achieved if you'd stayed committed to our career."

"Jesus Christ, it's like talking to a brick wall. I don't care about the accolades, the money, or the name. I don't even care that you lied to me all these years. All I care about is Vaughn's happiness. That's what you should be focusing on too."

"I am." He gestured to his shiny black car with tinted-out windows. "I want her to have the finer things in life. Things that my name and money can provide for her."

"That's just stuff, Joe. It's not happiness."

Chapter 23

The grandparents

"Are you sure about this? We can still turn back if you're not ready." Melissa turned to face Vaughn sitting in the backseat, staring out the window at the quaint weatherboard house at the back of the property. It was a modest home with a veranda that ran around the perimeter. Two weathered chairs sat beneath a window with a small round table between them, and at the other end was a swingseat. Pastures surrounded the little house. Cows grazed on the other side of the drive, and what looked like rows of fruit trees lined the back section. A small tractor sat idle in the middle of the green in front of the house.

"I'm okay." Vaughn smiled, her hand finding the door handle.

"I'll be right here if you need to have a break, okay?" Jane offered from the driver's seat.

"You sure you don't want to come in?" Melissa asked. "I feel bad making you sit out here by yourself."

"I'm a big girl. I'll be fine. I have a trashy magazine to read." She waved it in the air. "This is your time."

As they walked up the gravel drive, the front door swung open and a woman with silver hair hanging loose around her face stepped out. She wore a long flowing skirt with gumboots peeking out beneath. Behind her, a tall willowy man followed, holding a hand in the air in welcome. His skin was tanned and leathery, and his hair was jet black with flecks of grey.

Melissa stopped in front of the veranda, her hands slipping into the pockets at the back of her jeans. "Darlene, Ken." She nodded, offering a smile. "I'm Melissa, and this is Vaughn." She pulled her hand from her pocket, placing it on the small of Vaughn's back.

Tears filled Darlene's eyes as she brought her hands to her mouth. "Oh my." She glanced towards her husband, who had a similar look on his face. "She has his eyes."

Melissa cleared her throat. "Um *they*. Vaughn goes by they."

"Oh goodness, yes, that's right, you said on the phone. Sorry." She tapped a finger on her forehead. "I can be a bit forgetful sometimes."

Vaughn smiled, stepping forward. "It's okay."

"I'll remember from now on, I promise." She held her hands out, almost as if she were going to cup Vaughn's face. "Let me get a good look at you."

Vaughn raised her arms, palms up, doing a slow spin, and Darlene clamped her hands back over her mouth. She turned to Melissa. "They're beautiful. You've done a wonderful job."

"Thank you."

"Can I?" She opened her arms, looking to Vaughn for approval.

"Sure." Vaughn stepped into her embrace, their head resting below her chin. Darlene closed her eyes, stroking a hand down the back of Vaughn's head.

Ken placed his hand on his wife's back, watching on with a tearful smile.

"Oh, where are my manners?" Darlene pulled away, holding Vaughn's shoulders firmly. "Come inside, I'll rustle up some morning tea."

She led them through the front door and straight into a cosy sitting room. The mantlepiece was lined with framed photos of Joe at various stages of childhood. Vaughn made a beeline for them, picking one up and holding it out with a chuckle. "Dad had a mullet?"

"Oh yes." Darlene stood shoulder to shoulder with her, staring down at the smiling, blue-eyed boy with thick black hair cut short on the sides and long at the back. "He used to spike up the front too."

"Oh my god." Vaughn shook their head, eyes alight with mirth. "He's wearing fluorescent green and purple."

"It was a tracksuit set. Like what you'd wear on the ski fields. They were all the rage back then. All the kids had them." Darlene ran a finger lovingly over the picture.

"He'd never be caught dead in something like that now." Vaughn touched their hair, which now had blue at the roots. "He hates all the colours I put in my hair."

145

Darlene tsked. "You should take this and remind him how he dressed as a kid. He was always trying to stand out."

"Yeah, life on the land didn't suit him much, did it, love?" Ken's voice was gruff as he lowered himself into a well-worn armchair complete with multi-coloured crochet blanket draped over the back.

"No, it didn't." Her voice was clipped, her expression tight. Then like a cloud passing the sun, it was gone. She smiled, slapping her hands against her thighs. "Right. Who wants a coffee?"

She bustled off to the kitchen, boiling the jug and putting together a plate of cookies and slices.

Ken sniffed, patting the chair beside him. "You have to excuse my wife. Joseph's leaving was hard on her. She never gave up hoping he'd come back."

Melissa took the seat beside him. "I can only imagine how hard that must've been."

"It was a shock, that's for sure. Though I suppose we should've seen it coming. He never was interested in how things ran around here. Always looking for the next best thing. Always wanting what he couldn't have was our Joseph." He shook his head, staring into the distance. "Damn near broke her heart when she found his room cleared out."

"Wow, harsh." Vaughn frowned. "He didn't even say goodbye?"

"Not a word. One day he was home for dinner, the next he was gone." His right hand gripped the arm of the chair, his knuckles turning white. "We weren't

146

well off, still aren't, but we made sure he didn't want for things. Still wasn't enough for him though."

Darlene swept in with a tray, placing it on the coffee table. "Help yourself to something to eat." She handed Ken a steaming mug of coffee, then tipped a spoonful of sugar in another and topped it up with milk. "I wasn't sure how you had yours." She sat opposite Ken, gesturing for Melissa and Vaughn to make themselves a drink.

"Thank you. This is lovely." Melissa took a slice of brownie and sat back. "You have a beautiful home."

"All thanks to Darlene here," Ken said, giving her a smile that made her blush.

"You old charmer you." She waved a hand, a smile gracing her lips. "The orchard is much more impressive than in here."

"I thought I saw fruit trees out the back. What do you grow?"

"Apricots and peaches. Best damn fruit you'll ever taste." Ken winked. "Darlene keeps busy all summer making jams and fruit crumbles." He raised a finger in the air, as if he'd just had an idea. "You should take some home with you. See what you think."

"Maybe you could come and help me this summer, Vaughn. I could always use an extra pair of hands." Darlene glanced nervously at Melissa. "If that's okay?"

"Of course. I wouldn't mind coming along myself. I've never been able to master jam making."

"Oh wonderful." Darlene beamed. "The more the merrier."

"Did Dad help when he was younger?" Vaughn asked, and Darlene's smile disappeared.

"No, not really. He didn't see the point in spending the time making jam when it could be bought from the store in less time." She shrugged. "City life was always more his thing."

Ken made a noise in the back of his throat, and Darlene shot him a look before continuing. "He never really fit in with the other boys his age around here. Most were busy on the family farms, learning the ropes, but not our Joseph. He was more interested in how he could streamline things and turn it into profit."

Ken scoffed. "He wanted to be a big shot, and we didn't fit that picture. That Balderson fella gave him what we couldn't, and he didn't look back."

"Ken," Darlene scolded.

"Darlene. You know it's true."

"Well." She fluffed her skirt about her knees, avoiding his gaze. Turning her attention to Vaughn, she reached out and took her hand. "What about you? What do you like doing?"

"Um, I like to draw."

Melissa rolled her eyes. "That's an understatement. Vaughn is a talented artist. The Sweetwater Youth put on a show a few months ago, and Vaughn was responsible for the majority of the set design, and at the moment, they're working on a mural."

"Oh how lovely. I do love the arts. Where is this mural? We'd love to see it, wouldn't we, Ken?"

"Yes, of course."

"Um, it's not quite finished yet, but—" they glanced at their mother, "—there's going to be an unveiling when it's done."

"There is? You didn't tell me that."

"I'm telling you now." Vaughn grinned. "And we only discussed it the other day. Shane Smith is coming in to put up some scaffold so I can finish the top." They turned back to Darlene and Ken. "It's been covered up for weeks now, so no one has been able to see it. Not even Mum." She grinned wickedly.

"Well, you can count us in. Make sure you send us an invite."

Vaughn's face split into a wide grin, and Melissa's heart warmed. Her own parents lived a plane ride away, and they only got to see them once or twice a year. It hurt her to think how much time Darlene and Ken had missed out on with Vaughn, especially living so close, and all because Joe had a misguided notion of what was important.

How could he ever have thought that money and a reputation meant more than family?

Chapter 24

The courtroom

Melissa sucked in a deep breath, letting it out slowly. She was dressed in a pinstriped skirt that sat just below the knee, and one of Jane's tapered jackets over a plain mauve shirt. Her hair was pulled back into a bun, her make-up subdued. Beside her, Vaughn paced, chewing their thumb. It had taken two weeks for them to come up with a statement they were happy with, but now that the day had arrived, nerves were taking over.

"What if he hates me?"

"Oh, honey, why would you say that?

"Because I'm choosing you over him." Their lip trembled.

"You're his daughter. He could never hate you. I know it doesn't seem like it, but he's doing what he thinks is best for you." She brushed her hand over Vaughn's cheek. "All you can do is be honest and true to yourself. No one can fault you for that."

"Your mum's right. You've got this, kid." Jane bumped her fist with Vaughn's. "And I'll be right there too for moral support."

"Thanks." Vaughn leaned their head into Jane's chest. They'd formed an even closer connection over the past month, Jane lending a sympathetic ear when needed, or a bit of comic relief when tensions were high.

Melissa was grateful for her presence. She'd been somewhat of a rock to them both while the court case had been looming. She took Jane's hand, holding it tight to her side. "Thank you for being here."

"I wouldn't be anywhere else. My girls need me." She flashed one of her over-confident smiles. "Everything will be fine. You'll see." Her attention turned to the hall behind Melissa, and she leaned in. "Looks like you've got some more supporters."

Melissa turned to see Darlene and Ken striding towards them. They'd left their gumboots at home and dressed in their Sunday best. Darlene waved, her smile warm and motherly. Melissa very nearly cried at the sight of her. There hadn't been enough time for her own parents to arrange a flight to be with them, but they'd spent many hours on the phone in the lead-up. Still, having Darlene and Ken there as surrogate parents meant the world to her.

"We thought you could do with the company." Darlene pulled her in for a hug.

"Thank you."

"No, thank you. We may have lost our son, but we've gained a granddaughter and daughter-in-law. We're ever so thankful to you for allowing us to be part of your lives." She reached for Vaughn, wrapping her arms around her. "How're you holding up?"

"I'm okay, just nervous." Vaughn had reiterated to Melissa that they would not go with Joe, even if the courts ruled in his favour. She knew the conversation had been broached with Darlene about them possibly going to stay with them on the farm until things settled.

"I know, sweetheart, but it'll all be over soon. Just this one last hurdle." She kissed their forehead, then used her thumb to wipe the dab of lipstick she'd left there.

Clipped heels sounded down the hall, and Robyn appeared around the corner. "They're ready for us." She motioned for Melissa and Vaughn to follow her. "The character references will remain out here until they're called for. Darlene and Ken are family, so if you'd like them present, they're welcome to sit at the back of the room."

Melissa reached back for Jane's hand.

"I'm here," Jane whispered as they slipped into the room. She gave her hand one last squeeze before letting go and joining Darlene and Ken.

When Joe heard them enter, he turned, his eyes widening as he took in the sight of his parents with Jane. His jaw worked. Melissa raised her chin, striding to the front without a second glance at him. A surge of confidence coursed through her, knowing he was unsettled by their unexpected presence.

She took up her spot beside Robyn, and they waited while the judge entered the room and took his seat. He was an older man with a grandfatherly face, creased around the eyes and mouth, as if he'd spent a lifetime laughing. Wire-rimmed spectacles perched on the bridge of his nose, and he kept pushing them back with his forefinger. He addressed the court and asked both lawyers to state their names and client's names.

Joe was called to give his statement first. He stood, ramrod straight, and cleared his throat several times before speaking. His normally cool, calm and collected public façade was shaken, and he appeared flustered and stumbled over his words. He explained his reasoning for calling the hearing, but it sounded weak even to his own ears. Still, he carried on, laying out exactly how he felt.

When he'd finished, the judge nodded for him to take a seat, and then turned his attention to Melissa. Robyn gave her an encouraging smile, sliding her a slip of paper with four words scrawled across it. *Speak from the heart.*

She had a whole spiel worked out about how Joe wasn't who he said he was and how he had disowned his own family, but upon seeing him so flummoxed, she couldn't do it to him. Instead, she spoke of the challenges of raising a child on your own, the close bond she had with Vaughn, and that, unlike Joe, she wanted to see Vaughn succeed in her chosen field and not force them to be something they're not. That she valued truth above everything, and Vaughn was only being true to themself. She finished off by saying thank you to the court for allowing her to say her piece.

"And you, Siobhan? You're of an age where you can make decisions for yourself. How do you feel about it all?" the judge asked, gesturing for them to stand.

There was a screech as their chair scraped across the ground, and Vaughn's cheeks flushed. "Sorry."

The judge waved them on.

"Well," they started, chancing a glance at their father, who sat with his back rigid against the seat, staring to the front of the room. He wouldn't even look at them. "Your honour, um, for the record, it's Vaughn. I don't go by Siobhan."

The judge looked down at the paperwork in front of him. "My apologies, Vaughn, continue."

Vaughn let out a slow breath. "I love my father." They glanced across at him again. Still nothing. "But I wish to stay with my mum, Melissa Hobart." They raked a hand through their hair. "I can't be the person he wants me to be, and I don't think I should have to change who I am for his happiness. Family is meant to love unconditionally, and I have that with my mum and Jane, and my grandparents, who I only just met." They turned to Darlene and Ken, who gave a smile and a thumbs up.

Joe scoffed, folding his arms across his chest and turning his head to the side.

The judge frowned. "Please refrain from further outbursts, Mr. Balderson. You had your chance to speak." He turned his attention back to Vaughn, his face softening. "Please continue."

"My father thinks I'm incapable of making decisions about my future because of my age, and he won't accept me as I am. As non-binary." They sucked their bottom lip in, once again turning to Joe. "Dad, I don't want you dictating how I live my life. Yes, I might make mistakes or fail. In fact, I'm bound to. But at least I will have tried." They took a breath. "I just want you to see me for me. I'm not interested in business, or parties, or pretty dresses. I like the way I dress, and the name I've chosen for myself. I like who I am. I just want you to like who I am too." A tear slid down their face, and they swiped it away before dragging their eyes back to the judge. "That's all, your honour."

"Thank you, Vaughn. You're a most articulate speaker." The judge shuffled through the pages in front of him. "I see here this isn't the first legal custody arrangement?"

Robyn stood. "That's right, your honour. When the complainant and defendant separated in 2009 a custody arrangement was filed by Mr. Balderson."

"And you were happy to acquiesce at the time?" The judge lowered his glasses, staring at Joe. "Is that correct?"

"I wouldn't say I was happy about it, your honour."

The judge sighed, swiping his glasses from his face and pinching the bridge of his nose. "But you did not contest the agreement, is that correct?"

"That is correct. I believed Melissa to be capable at the time."

"So you trusted her to have full custody of your daughter for thirteen years and only now believe her to be unfit because of her decision to form a relationship with a woman. Is that correct?"

"That's not the only reason, your honour."

"But it was one of the deciding factors."

"Yes." The judge lowered his brows, and Joe cleared his throat. "Your honour."

"Am I to believe then that you have not entered any similar relationships with women while your daughter has been present?"

Joe's mouth opened and closed; his cheeks flushed. "I don't see how that's relevant."

"You don't see how it's relevant that you yourself have entered into relationships with women while your daughter has been around, while you disagree with the mother of your child doing the same?"

"Ah." Joe tugged at his collar.

"And you state that Vaughn isn't old enough to know who they are and have clearly been brainwashed, yet I see in front of me, a confident, capable person who knows exactly who they are. You don't become that without the care of good parents. Mr. Balderson, I believe you when you say you want what's best, but I think you need to reconsider that *your* idea of what's best and Vaughn's differ. They say that children are an extension of ourselves, but that doesn't mean they have to mirror us. In fact, the sign of a good parent is one who allows their child the freedom to grow and become who they want to be. I understand it can be difficult to see them make what we deem to be mistakes, but that is how they learn."

"I don't need you to explain things to me as if I'm a simpleton. Do you know who I am? What I do?" He shook his head with disdain.

"I know perfectly well who you are, *Mr. Balderson*. But it seems you have forgotten to whom you are speaking." He levelled Joe with a stare. "Take a seat."

Joe's wide-eyed stare at being reprimanded made him seem vulnerable, childlike. Melissa almost felt sorry for him. It was probably the first time anyone had spoken to him that way in a long time. All the same, she gave Robyn the nod. It was time.

Robyn stood. "If I may, your honour." She flapped a sheet of paper in the air. "It appears even Mr. Balderson doesn't know who he is." She rounded the desk, handing the judge Joe's birth certificate, change of name, and details of the real Mr. Balderson's death.

Joe's complexion turned pallid.

"He talks of Vaughn not being able to make decisions about their own life, when he was barely a year older when he made the biggest decision of his life; to change his name and cut off his parents."

There was a sniffle from the back of the room. Melissa felt a stab in her heart, knowing what this would be doing to Darlene and Ken. Dredging up the past was never kind on anyone.

"Your honour, that's entirely different circumstances and of no relevance." Joe jumped to his feet before his attorney could stop him.

"Sit down," he hissed, but Joe waved him off.

"None of that has anything to do with Siobhan and what's best for her. I'd like it removed from the record."

The judge removed his glasses, pointing them at Joe's attorney. "Keep your client under control."

"Yes, your honour." His eyes pleaded with Joe, who finally acquiesced with a sigh.

158

"Your honour, my client didn't want to use this information, but under the circumstances…" Robyn let her words hang in the air.

The judge turned to Melissa. "Thank you for bringing this to my attention, though I don't believe it will make a difference to the proceedings. I've seen enough." He gathered up the papers, putting them into a pile. "I understand you have brought character references here with you today, but I don't believe that's necessary. I've read the written statements each has provided, and I see no reason to take this any further. Vaughn is happy in your care, and from what I can see, you've done a fabulous job raising a strong, independent person. If you're happy to, I'll leave the custody arrangement as it is; Vaughn remains full time in your care with fortnightly visitation awarded to Joseph Balderson, and at Vaughn's discretion, of course, along with any extra you deem appropriate." Raising the gavel, he brought it down with a resounding crack. "Court is adjourned."

Chapter 25

The aftermath

A collective sigh of relief filled the room as the judge left the chamber and everyone stood. Jane rushed to the front, practically leaping over the barrier and wrapping both Melissa and Vaughn in a firm hug. "I knew you'd have nothing to worry about." Her trembling hands said otherwise.

When she let go, Melissa took hold of Robyn's hand, grasping it between both of hers. "I can't thank you enough for getting us through this."

"You did all the hard work. I just guided you."

"Still, I would've been a nervous wreck without you beside me." She turned to Vaughn, taking them by the shoulders and looking them up and down. "When did you become so grown up?" She pulled them in close, inhaling the scent of their hair. "I'm so proud of you."

"Thanks. I'm kinda proud of me too." They huffed out a laugh. "I didn't think I'd be able to get the words out."

Melissa smoothed her hand across Vaughn's hair, kissing the top of their head. "You did great."

"I think we should have a celebratory lunch," Jane said, swinging her arms around both their shoulders. "What do you think?"

"Sounds perfect. Robyn, you want to join us?" Melissa asked as Robyn filed papers away in her briefcase.

"Thanks for the offer, but I'm due back in court tomorrow morning and I need to get on the road." She clasped her hands in front of her. "Raincheck?"

"Absolutely. Thanks again."

Robyn gave a quick incline of her head before striding out of the room.

"What about you two?" Melissa beckoned to Joe's parents. "Would you like to join us for lunch?"

Darlene's eyes sparkled with tears as she stared at the back of her son. Joe's head was bowed, his hands steepled against the table. He had the look of a man defeated.

"That would be lovely. I think Darlene just needs a minute," Ken answered, wrapping his arm tightly around his wife's waist.

"Of course."

Darlene pulled away, edging closer to Joe, her gnarled fingers reaching towards him. Her hand closed around his forearm, and his eyes dragged from the table to where she held him.

"Joseph," she whispered under her breath. "It's good to see you, son."

Joe snorted derisively. "I'm sure it's not. You don't have to pretend. I'm an adult. I can take it."

"I'm not pretending. It *is* good to see you." Her voice caught in her throat, and Joe seemed to hesitate before once again hardening his expression. "I'm sure I'm an even bigger disappointment to you now."

Darlene gasped, her hand flying to her mouth. "How could you say that? You were never a disappointment. Never."

"Let's not beat around the bush. I wasn't what you hoped for in a son; someone to take over the farm and run the land." He held his hands up, twisting them front to back. "I don't like getting my hands dirty. I like the finer things in life. I never fit into your world." His eyes widened on those last words, and his gaze flitted to Vaughn.

His shoulders seemed to concave, and he shuddered. If Darlene didn't know any better, she could've sworn his lower lip was trembling.

"You have a beautiful family," she said quickly. "Vaughn is a treasure."

Joe's head dropped further, his eyes squinched closed. "She is."

"I think you mean they." She patted his arm. "You need to accept that."

He raked his hand through his hair, leaving it sticking up on end.

"I know." He sounded defeated, like all fight had left his body. "It's just—" he peered over at Vaughn, "—I can't wrap my head around it. It doesn't make sense to me."

"It doesn't have to make sense to you though, as long as it makes sense to them. You just have to roll with it. Show them you care no matter what."

"I've never been good at rolling with it. I'm more of a follow the rules kind of guy."

She smiled. "I remember."

163

"There are no rules for this. I'm out of my depth. How do I stop thinking of her as my little girl?"

"I don't think they expect you to get it right all the time, just try, son. That's all you can do. Kids need to know their parents are on their side." She paused, her voice ragged. "But then, I guess you never felt that from us either."

His brow creased. "It's not…" He shook his head, wrestling with his emotions. "I don't know." He stared at the judge's pulpit, his eyes dancing back and forth. "I thought I was meant for more, but—" he waved his hand towards Vaughn and Melissa, who were wrapped in each other's arms, "—it appears my idea of a good life is skewed. She's never like that with me."

"It's not too late, you know. There's still time to make things right." She tilted her head, taking his hand in hers. "Why don't you join us for lunch?"

"Oh no, I couldn't." He shook his head, wondering how he could've forgotten the comforting feel of his mother's hands. "I wouldn't want to impose."

"My sweet boy, did you not hear what Vaughn said? They love you, you wouldn't be imposing." She circled her thumb along the back of his hand. "And I would love to spend more time getting to know you again."

His eyes softened, and he squeezed her hand. "I'm sorry for leaving, Mum. Everything kind of snowballed and I went along with it. By the time I stopped for a breath, it had been years. I didn't think you'd want to see me."

"You're my son. I will *always* want to see you."

"Thank you, but I don't think Dad sees it the same way."

Ken was standing off to the side, his arms folded across his chest, his face set in a scowl as he watched their exchange.

"He'll come around. It's been hard on him. On both of us. But this is the time for all of us to have a second chance." She reached her weathered hand up to cup his jaw, and he closed his eyes, leaning in to her touch. "Think about it, okay?"

"I will." The group appeared to be gathering their things and making a move towards the exit. "You'd better go."

She gave his cheek a pat then let her hand slide from his face. Clutching her handbag in front of her, she joined the others.

Ken held the door open, ushering everyone out, but Vaughn stopped to wait for Darlene. "Is he okay?" They nodded towards Joe, who had slumped into a seat, his head in his hands. "He's struggling, but he'll come around."

With slow steps, Vaughn made their way back. "Dad?"

He raised his head, meeting their gaze with a sad smile. "Vaughn."

It was the first time he'd called them that. Vaughn sucked in a shaky breath. "I'm sorry if I hurt you by choosing Mum."

He shook his head, bracing his hands on the rail in front of him. "I understand why you did." He let out a sigh. "I'm sorry too."

"It's okay."

"No, it isn't. You were right, what you said earlier. I should never have expected you to be anything other than who you are." He reached out, running his thumb along their jaw. "You've always been my little girl, it's hard to see you as anything else. I know I haven't been the most forthcoming with my emotions, but I do love you."

"I love you too."

"It's going to take me some time to get used to this whole—" he waved his hand through the air, "—no gender thing, but I'd like to try, if you'll let me."

Vaughn's lips curled into a wide smile. "Of course, Dad." They flung their arms around him, burying their head in his chest. Joe slowly enfolded them in his arms, resting his chin on their head.

"So, how does this work exactly? Can I still call you my daughter?"

Vaughn chuckled. "Yeah, that's fine."

"And you're set on Vaughn?"

They nodded. "I am."

"And the hair?"

Vaughn grinned up at him. "The hair is staying too. Well, it might change to a different colour. Maybe hot pink next?"

Joe grimaced. "Can you give me a minute to get used to the blue and green before you add any more colours?"

166

"I guess I can manage that." Vaughn glanced to the end of the room where Melissa stood waiting. She was swiping a finger beneath her eyes. Vaughn turned back to their father. "We're going out for lunch. Why don't you come too?"

"Are you sure?"

"Yeah, Dad. It'll be like old times."

Joe snorted. "I haven't been out for a meal with you and your mother since you were two years old. You can't possibly remember that."

"Maybe not, but I have a very active imagination." They tapped their head. "It's all up here."

"I suppose that comes part and parcel with the art thing."

Vaughn nodded. "It does." They took hold of his hand, tugging him to his feet. "Come on. Mum won't mind."

He glanced up to see Melissa watching them from the door. She had a warm smile on her face, and a tear in her eye. "Are you sure?"

Vaughn followed his gaze and waved a dismissive hand. "Oh yeah, those are happy tears. Totally different to sad tears." They pulled on his hand again. "Come on."

He followed after them, all the while giving Melissa an apologetic look.

"It's okay if Dad comes to lunch, right? Vaughn said as soon as they were level with her.

Melissa's mouth opened and closed a few times. She and Joe hadn't had a civilised conversation in years, let alone a meal together, but the eager smile on

Vaughn's face could convince her of anything. "I don't see why not."

Vaughn turned to Joe with a smirk. "Told you."

He cleared his throat. "Thank you, Melissa. I appreciate this."

"As long as Vaughn's happy, I'm happy."

"Yes. Of course." He nodded, shoving his free hand in his pocket. "Look, uh… I want to apologise for dragging you through all this. It shouldn't have taken a judge, my mother, daughter, and you to convince me I was putting my own needs first." He cleared his throat again, scrutinising the floor at his feet. "I was wrong."

Melissa gawped at him, her mouth giving a good impression of a goldfish. "Uh, who are you and what have you done with my ex-husband?"

Joe glanced up at her with a half-smile. "I suppose I deserve that."

She folded her arms across her chest. "Yeah, you do, and not just for Vaughn either."

"I know I've not been fair to you—"

"I'm not talking about me," she interrupted. "I'm talking about your parents. You destroyed your mother when you left. And you kept them from their granddaughter."

He had the decency to look ashamed. "I know."

Melissa reached out and squeezed his wrist. "Money isn't everything. Sure, it can buy you nice things, but it doesn't keep you warm at night or make you feel loved. Family is worth so much more than anything money can buy."

"I'm beginning to see that." He smiled down at Vaughn, his hand still firmly within their grasp. "And I intend on making a concerted effort this time. Starting with…" He pulled his wallet from his pocket, sifting through the notes and handing Melissa a wad. "I believe I owe you this."

She frowned at the money. "Don't get me wrong, a handful of cash is always nice, but, uh, what's this for exactly?"

"For the suit. For the formal? You asked if I could help out." He glanced between the two of them, his mouth set in a tight line. "Or am I too late?"

Chapter 26

The formal

"Oh my gosh," Melissa gushed. "You both look gorgeous!" She clapped, pulling her phone from her pocket to snap a few shots of Vaughn and their best friend, Mackenzie. They had decided to make a statement and go to the formal together. Vaughn had on their one-of-a-kind Giancarlo masterpiece, complete with fresh matching green highlights in their hair. Mackenzie wore an ankle-length dress of silver that shimmered under the lights. Her hair was pulled into a French twist, and long silver earrings dangled from her ears. They made a striking couple.

"You are going to turn heads, that's for sure." Jane watched from the side with a glass of wine in her hand.

"That's kind of the point," Mackenzie said with a wink. "We're paving the way for other non-traditional couples."

Jane tilted her glass in a salute. "I like your style. We weren't allowed same sex couples or anything other than boy and girl at my formal. I ended up going with my friend's older brother, and we barely spoke two words to each other." She snorted. "I don't even remember his name. We just wanted the cheaper tickets." She shook her head, taking a sip of her wine. "Good times."

"It is allowed, but they don't encourage it."

"Yeah, when they talk about the formal, they only mention traditional couples, but there actually isn't anything to say it's not allowed, so we thought we'd lead the charge and be the first." Vaughn grinned.

"I think it's a great thing you're doing. You never know who might see the two of you and realise it's okay for them to do the same." Melissa brushed down the shoulders of Vaughn's jacket. "I'm proud of you both for making a stand."

Gravel crunched outside, and the bright headlights of Joe's Mercedes shone in through the window as he parked.

"Looks like your ride is here. You all ready to go?" Melissa fluffed about with Vaughn's jacket a little more before Jane took her hand and pulled her away.

"They're fine," she murmured.

"Have you got your phone to call when you need picked up?"

"It's in my pocket." Vaughn opened one side of her jacket to reveal a secret pocket with their phone buttoned in.

There was a knock at the door, and Vaughn raced over to open it. "Hey, Dad." They smiled, holding their hands out wide. "What do you think?"

"Wow." Joe stepped into the small entryway, closing the door behind him. "That's quite some suit. Am I allowed to say you look beautiful in it?"

Vaughn snorted. "Of course, because I do." They gripped the lapels, pulling them tight. "And this is Mackenzie, my date." They held their tongue between their teeth as they gestured to the beauty in silver.

Mackenzie appraised him with a cold stare, her arms folded across her chest. She still hadn't forgiven him for the way he treated Vaughn.

Joe bowed his head to her. "What a beautiful dress."

"Thanks," she said in a clipped tone.

"Right. Well." He looked to Melissa for help, but all she did was shrug. He was on his own. "Shall we go then?" He wrenched the door open, ushering them into the night air.

"Bye, Mum," Vaughn called out as they ran out the door with a wave.

"Bye! Have fun!"

"But not too much fun!" Jane added as an afterthought, then sniggered. "I've always wanted to say that."

"Remind them to call if they want to be picked up before the after party."

Joe nodded. "I will."

"And remind them not to take any drinks from strangers."

"It's a school formal, Mel, not a nightclub." Jane rolled her eyes, even though she too had been thinking the same thing.

"In fact, just tell them not to drink anything."

Joe raised his brow. "I don't know that that's a good idea. Dehydration is a serious thing."

"Okay, they can drink water that they get for themselves."

The horn blasted from the drive. "Come on, Dad! We want to get there while the red carpet is still out."

Joe's eyes widened. "Red carpet?"

"Oh yeah, they go all out at these things now. Announcements and spotlights. It's a whole thing." Jane refilled her glass with a glint in her eye. "Did they even have formals back when you were at school, Joseph?" She'd taken to calling him that ever since he joined them for lunch after court. "Or was everything still in black and white then?"

Melissa stifled a laugh behind her hand, while Joe pretended to ignore her.

"Dad!"

"I'd better get going before they leave without me." He ducked out the door, pulling it closed behind him.

Melissa went to the window, watching as they pulled out onto the road. Two quick beeps rang out, and she raised her hand in a wave.

"They're going to be fine." Jane pressed her chest to Melissa's back, wrapping her hands around her waist. "They're both mature enough to keep out of trouble."

"I know." That's what she was afraid of. "They're growing up so fast."

"I hear that happens."

"Sometimes I wish I could freeze time, you know? Just to have them still need me for a little longer."

Jane gripped Melissa's waist, spinning her until they were face-to-face. "They're always going to need you."

"Not in the same capacity."

"No, but that's a good thing. It means you did a great job as a parent." Her fingers squeezed, pulling her hips in close. "And it means you can spend more time on other things." Her hands slid down Melissa's curves, her head ducking low enough to nuzzle against her nose. "Other needs." She brushed her lips against the bow of Melissa's mouth. "Wants, even."

With a low groan, Melissa slid her hands up and into the hair at the nape of Jane's neck, her breath ragged. She pushed onto her toes, pressing her lips to Jane's in a searing kiss.

Jane crushed her back against the wall, hitching one leg up over her hip. Her tongue laved down the length of Melissa's throat, dipping below the collar of her shirt.

Melissa arched her back, her fingers gripping Jane's hair as she took one pert nipple in her mouth. With nimble fingers, Jane unbuttoned Melissa's shirt, her lips blazing a trail of heat with every bit of flesh exposed.

Jane undid the last button, letting the fabric pool on the floor as she reached for the zip of Melissa's jeans. These too fell to the floor, wrapped around her ankles, and Jane, dropping to her knees, grazed her palms up the length of each leg, tracing every contour until she reached the apex of Melissa's thighs. She let out a whimper, widening her legs ever so slightly.

Nudging the flimsy cotton of her panties aside, Jane ran a finger through her slick folds. Her free hand curled around to grip the soft flesh of Melissa's arse, holding her in place as she lapped at the tight bud between her thighs.

Melissa flung her head back against the wall, one hand tangled in Jane's hair, the other splayed against the wall. Her legs threatened to buckle beneath her with every flick of Jane's tongue, and her hips moved of their own volition, chasing the high that was already so close she couldn't think straight.

Jane added a second finger, curling them up to find the rough ridge inside, and Melissa gasped, her hips jolting forward.

"Oh god, yes!" She couldn't think, could barely breathe the build-up was so intense. Her eyes squeezed shut, her thighs tensed, and all her nerve endings zeroed in on the one spot as Jane flattened her tongue and took long, languishing laps.

Melissa panted, her cries loud in the quiet room. And when she reached the pinnacle, her mouth dropped open in a silent scream of pleasure.

Jane sat back on her haunches, licking her lips with a salacious grin. Melissa's legs turned to jelly, and she slid to the floor, her jeans still around her ankles.

"That was… I have no words."

"Oh, I got you. Earth shattering? Mind blowing? The best you've ever had?" Jane waggled her brows, running a lazy finger along Melissa's hips and leaving a trail of goosebumps in her wake. "Legendary, even?"

Melissa snickered, curling herself around Jane and sinking her teeth into the soft flesh of her thigh.

"Oh." She drew the word out. "You want to play rough?" She took advantage of Melissa's bound legs and straddled her, pinning her arms above her head with a wicked grin. "Two can play at that."

Chapter 27

The unveiling

Swarms of people milled about outside the Sweetwater Youth rooms. Newspapers had been hung across the windows for the past few weeks to stop people from peeking inside before the big unveiling, and it seemed to have intrigued the masses enough for them to step out on a bright but brisk Saturday morning.

Vaughn had been down at the centre every day after school and in weekends adding the final touches, and last night Shane had removed the scaffolding and rigged a makeshift curtain across the wall.

Melissa was both nervous and excited. Nervous because she knew how much it meant to Vaughn, but excited to finally see what they'd been working so hard on for months. She and Jane had awoken early and made a special breakfast of pancakes with bacon and maple syrup to celebrate the big day, but Vaughn had been too nervous to eat more than a few bites.

After pulling every item of clothing out of their wardrobe and tossing it on the bed, they'd finally come out dressed in a pair of stonewash overalls with one strap hanging behind their back, a black tank top with splashes of colour all over it, and their Doc Martens. Their green and blue hair was slicked back on the sides and spiked up on top, and a chunky chain looped around their neck and attached to their right ear.

Now, standing outside the youth centre with everyone else, their face had drained of colour. "I wasn't expecting this many people."

Melissa rubbed her hands up and down Vaughn's arms encouragingly. "You need to get used to it. There will be even more vying for your attention when you hold your first exhibit at an art gallery."

"And I'll be the first one in line to buy a Vaughn Balderson original, and I'll tell everyone I knew them before they became rich and famous," Jane added, playfully punching Vaughn's arm. "I expect mates' rates too."

Vaughn laughed. "You got it."

"Hey, guys." Raoul marched up, his eyes dancing across the already large crowd. "Great turnout." He rubbed his hands together. "You ready for this?"

"I guess." Vaughn shrugged. "Kinda have to be, don't I?"

"Nervous?" he asked, giving her a sympathetic smile. Speaking in public had never been something he enjoyed at their age. In fact, it still wasn't his favourite thing to do. He preferred to leave that kind of showboating to Giancarlo and Lucious.

"A little." Vaughn swallowed, peering around the sea of faces.

"Don't be." He grabbed hold of her wrist, giving it a squeeze. "From what I've seen of it already, it's nothing short of a miracle. You've transformed the

180

whole room, making it bright and vivacious. You have a real knack for this, Vaughn. You're going to go far."

Melissa swiped a tear from her eyes, chuckling when Vaughn gave her a wide-eyed stare. "I'm just so proud of you, and hearing Raoul say how talented you are… it makes my heart sing." She clutched a hand to her chest.

Vaughn snorted. "Okay. They drew the word out.

"You'll understand one day."

Lucious poked his head out the door. "It's all ready." He grinned, giving Vaughn a wink before closing the door again.

"Well." Raoul clapped his hands. "Looks like it's show time." He turned to the crowd, clearing his throat. "If I could have your attention, please?"

A hush fell over the gathering, and a camera flashed from somewhere near the back.

"My name is Raoul Montgomery, and I am the coordinator of the Sweetwater Youth. Earlier this year, I tasked one of our youths with a challenge. To transform the centre with their art. That youth was Vaughn Balderson." He moved his hand to the small of their back, inching them forward. "I noticed their talents from the very start when I witnessed children piled around them asking for pictures. Vaughn drew whatever they asked for, and drew it well.

"If you were lucky enough to come along to our mid-year performance of *A Midsummer Night's Dream*, you would have seen some of their handy work in the set design too.

Over the past few months, Vaughn has spent much of their time here designing and painting, and we're finally ready to share it." He beamed down at Vaughn as the crowd began to clap.

Melissa and Jane were bouncing on the balls of their feet, clapping the loudest. With her hands around her mouth, Mackenzie bellowed out an exuberant "woo!", and Jane tucked her fingers between her lips, whistling loudly.

Chuckling, Raoul held his hands up to silence them. "The doors will be open in but a moment, and I encourage you to examine every detail of Vaughn's work. It's quite remarkable." He turned to the window and tapped three times.

The door swung open and Lucious stepped out at the same time as the newspapers were torn down from the inside of the window.

"Right this way, folks." Lucious stepped aside, securing the door to the wall.

Raoul ushered Vaughn inside first, leading them towards the large black curtain covering the mural. "Enjoy it," he whispered, stepping back and giving them the spotlight.

Vaughn cleared their throat, looking around the room that suddenly felt tiny with so many people squashed inside. Their mum and Jane stood to the side with Raoul and Lucious, all with Cheshire grins on their faces.

As they opened their mouth to speak, there was a commotion outside, and a frantic tapping on the glass as Darlene's face peered in. "We're here!" she called out. "Don't start without us!"

Vaughn chuckled as a pathway opened and Darlene dragged Ken behind her. "Sorry," she huffed, adjusting her handbag on her shoulder. "This one wanted to take the scenic route." She rolled her eyes. "I told him there wasn't enough time." She tutted, then grabbed hold of Vaughn and folded them into her arms. "I'm so glad we made it. Looks like half the town is here."

"Yeah. It's kinda crazy they're here to see me… or what I've done, I suppose." They laughed nervously.

"It's not crazy at all." Darlene kissed her on the cheek then rubbed her thumb over the same spot. "I'm so proud of you."

"Thanks… Grandma." Vaughn shrunk into themselves, as if they weren't sure it was okay to call her that.

Tears welled in Darlene's eyes, and she nodded, unable to form words.

"Vaughn?" It was Raoul, nodding towards the curtain. It was time.

On shaky legs, Vaughn moved to stand in front of the pulley Shane had set up. It was rigged to first lift from the bottom and then all at once fall to the floor to reveal the mural in all its glory. All Vaughn had to do was give it a tug.

The room quietened, and Vaughn closed their eyes, taking a deep breath in through their nose and huffing it out through their mouth. "Ah, hi everybody," they started. "As Raoul said, I'm Vaughn, but he got the last name wrong." They looked over at Melissa with a smile. "It's Vaughn Hobart."

Melissa's hand flew to the base of her throat, and she stifled a sob.

Vaughn cleared their throat. "I'd like to thank you all for coming to see the unveiling of my mural. I honestly thought it was just going to be my family here, so I'm kind of blown away by how many of you there are."

The audience laughed, and Vaughn grinned, loosening up. "When Raoul asked me if I'd be interested in doing this, I didn't even have to think twice. Art is my joy. It's what makes my heart sing—" they glanced at their mum with a smirk, "—as corny as that sounds. If I'm ever unsure or upset, art can lift me back up, and I hope that *my* art can do the same for others."

Melissa let out another muted sob and clapped her hands once before Jane wrapped her arms around her, holding her still.

Vaughn nodded at her. "That's my mum. She's the publisher and chief editor of The Sweetwater Gazette. She built it up from nothing. She's always told me I can do anything I put my mind to, and I think I'm finally starting to believe it." They smiled. "Thanks, Mum."

Melissa blew them a kiss, tears streaming down her face.

"And thank you to Raoul for giving me this opportunity and helping me realise my potential."

Raoul doffed an imaginary hat, tilting his head at them.

"Well, I guess it's time to show you all what you're here to see." They tugged on the pulley and the bottom pulled up revealing a splash of colour. The top of the curtain was next, sliding down the wall in slow motion to uncover Vaughn's masterpiece.

There was a collective gasp of appreciation, and then everyone started clapping and talking at once, pointing out different aspects.

Vaughn had made sure to include images of all the current kids of Sweetwater Youth doing what they love most. Mackenzie was holding fabric up to a mannequin with Giancarlo by her side. Kai was holding up the iconic happy and sad theatre masks. There was a group of boys dancing on strips of cardboard with a boombox beside them, while Katrina sang along to the music. There were mathematicians, gamers, sports players, everything. And right in the centre, holding everyone together, was Raoul.

"Oh my god, Vaughn, this is…" Melissa shook her head as she cast her gaze over the wall again. "This is amazing." She stared with open-mouthed wonder at her daughter.

"Thanks, Mum."

"Hey, kid," a familiar voice called from behind them. Robyn strode through the throngs of people milling about, holding her hand out to Vaughn. "That's some talent you've got there."

"I was going to say the same thing. Nice job, squirt." Shane ruffled Vaughn's hair, and his brother Adrian gave them a high five.

"Robyn, I didn't know you were coming." Melissa pulled her in for a hug.

"I could hardly miss it, not when I received a personalised invitation." She retrieved a card from her pocket and waved it in the air.

"Snap!" Darlene cried out, waving a similar card at Robyn. "We got one too."

Shane nudged Vaughn's arm. "Sorry we missed the big moment. Did it work okay?" He nodded to the crumpled curtain on the floor.

"Yeah, it was perfect, thank you." Vaughn gave him a beaming smile.

"Mum said to tell you she's sorry she couldn't make it. She's been having headaches again." He frowned, shoving his hands in his pockets.

"Oh, I hope she's okay."

"Yeah, she's tough as old boots. Had to be to raise us, right, Adrian?" He nudged his brother in the ribs, but Adrian wasn't paying any attention. His eyes were glued on the Amazonian woman talking to Vaughn's mum.

"Who is that?" he asked, tugging at his collar.

"That's Robyn. She's a lawyer from Brookhaven." Vaughn scrunched her nose. "I think Lucious said you all went to school together?"

Adrian dragged his gaze up her long legs. "Nah, I don't think so. I'd remember someone who looked like that."

"Put your tongue back in your mouth, bro. She's not from round here, and she's certainly out of your league," Shane scoffed. "Punching way above your weight there."

Adrian sniffed, squaring his shoulders. "You never know until you try, baby bro." He sauntered over, slotting himself in between Melissa and Robyn.

"What's he up to?" Lucious asked with a mischievous grin.

"Reckons he's gonna bag him that hot lawyer." Shane laughed, watching his brother work his magic.

Lucious snorted. "Is that so? This should be good."

"Why do I get the feeling I'm missing something?" Shane asked.

"You don't remember Robyn from school?"

Shane eyed her again before shaking his head. "Don't think so. What's her last name?"

Lucious smirked. "Hargreaves."

It was Shane's turn to snort. "The only Robyn Hargreaves I know was the captain of the first fifteen." He laughed, slapping his hand against Lucious's chest. "Can you imagine?"

"I can." Lucious quirked a brow, his lips curled into a grin.

Shane's eyes widened. "No." He flicked his gaze back over her. "No. It can't be."

Lucious nodded. "The one and the same."

Shane burst out laughing. "Wait till I tell Adrian!"

187

***

"There you are." Melissa sidled up to Vaughn, who was standing on tip toes scanning the room. "Who are you... Oh."

They dropped back to their heels, a frown creasing their brow and lips pursed. Melissa's heart sank. She hadn't seen him either.

Jane, picking up on the sudden mood change, took hold of Vaughn's hand, dragging them to the mural. "Is this who I think it is?" She pointed at an unmistakable likeness to Lucious handing Vaughn a sheet of wood in the shape of a tree for the woodland scenes of *A Midsummer Night's Dream*. Behind him was a tall woman in a pantsuit, with her hair pulled back from her face and a smirk on her lips. She was holding a piece of paper with 'M + J' scrawled in the centre and a heart around the outside.

Vaughn grinned up at her. "It's not Peter Parker, if that's what you're thinking."

"Of course not." Jane rolled her eyes. "He could never pull off that suit, or hairstyle, for that matter." She smoothed a hand over her slicked-back locks. "You did good, kid. This is seriously impressive."

"Thanks. I don't know what I'm going to do with my time now that it's done."

"I'm sure you'll think of something." She glanced over the top of Vaughn's head. "Looks like you're wanted over there." She spun Vaughn around, pointing out Joe as he strode their way with another man in tow.

"Vaughn." He took their hand, holding it against his chest. "This is outstanding." He ran his eyes over the mural, letting them linger on various points. "The colour, the vibrancy. I… I had no idea."

"I told you," Melissa said with a note of smugness.

"Yes. You've got quite the talent there," the other man spoke up, his smile warm and inviting. "I love the way you've combined mediums, giving the viewer a depth to each scene. It's really quite something."

Vaughn blinked, not knowing who this man was and why he was saying these things. "Um, thanks?"

"Sorry, where are my manners?" He held his hand out. "The name's Henry Schaefer. I'm the dean of St. Albert's School of Art."

Vaughn's eyes widened, and they gripped Melissa's hand. "You are?"

"I am, and I can say with not a word of a lie, you and your talents would be most welcome at our school. In fact, your youth coordinator, what was his name? Raoul?" Vaughn nodded, and he continued. "Yes, well, he contacted me a few weeks back, suggesting I might like to take a look. And then when Joe here reached out to me as well, I knew it was worth the trip to see for myself."

Melissa stared at Joe as if she'd never seen him before. He had been dead set against Vaughn attending art school for so long, she never in her wildest dreams imagined he would be the one to make the first call.

"Um, wow. Are you serious?" Vaughn looked from Henry to their father and back again.

"Absolutely."

"When you've finished high school, of course," Joe interjected, meeting Melissa's gaze. "I know I harp on about it, but an education is important." He eyed the busy design on the wall. "Even if you will most likely be tucked away in an art studio somewhere, only coming out for inspiration or exhibitions." He smiled, awkwardly tapping their shoulder with his fist. "You are incredible, and I'm sorry I didn't see it before."

Vaughn shrugged, and colour crept up their neck, giving them a glow. "It's okay."

"Henry, good to see you," Raoul said as he joined them. He took Henry's hand in his, giving a firm shake. "I was hoping you would make it."

"Yes, as am I. It's a great space you've got here. A lot of bare walls that could do with a splash of colour, don't you think, Vaughn?" He smiled warmly.

"You know, I have been working on an idea…"

Raoul chuckled good-naturedly. "That doesn't surprise me at all."

"Hey," Jane piped up. "Maybe you should do the ceiling next. You know, like Michelangelo. We could have Sweetwater Close's very own version of the Sistine Chapel right here."

Henry craned his neck back, taking in the bland white ceiling. "It certainly could do with a touch up. Though perhaps Vaughn might like to finish school first. After all, it did take Michelangelo the better part of five years to complete his work at the Vatican."

Jane almost choked on her drink. "Five years? On second thought, white is good. Makes the mural stand out."

All eyes were drawn back to the wall, with its blue and green bubble lettering and detailed caricatures. You could spend hours looking and still not find all the hidden easter eggs.

Melissa leant her head on Jane's shoulder, her arm snaking around her waist. "It's really quite something, isn't it?" she said with open pride.

Jane peered down at her, pressing her lips to the top of her head. "It sure is."

Acknowledgements

When I first started writing The Suitor, I hadn't planned on it becoming a series, but it quickly became clear I wasn't going to be able to leave the townsfolk of Sweetwater Close anytime soon. Melissa and Jane's story has been a fun one to write, not only because of Jane's crassness, but also because I got to revisit Vaughn's character and explore their non-binary role. As you've probably guessed, I'll be focusing on Robyn and Adrian in the next book.

As always, I must thank my friend and editor, Trina. Thank you for listening to me waffle on about my books and constantly updating you on my progress. I honestly don't think I'd still be doing this if it weren't for you.

To my writing buddies, Debs and Indi. Without you two pushing me and writing alongside me, I wouldn't have met my deadline. I can't thank you enough for sticking with me.

To Nicole, for always being my sounding board and encouraging me to both procrastinate and write at the same time! Our constant updates are what keep me going.

And, of course, to my readers. Thank you for joining me on this journey and taking a chance on my books. And a special thanks to those of you who have left reviews. It means the world to me to hear how much you enjoy my stories. It's what makes all the editing woes worth it!

I'm thoroughly enjoying bringing the town of Sweetwater Close to life, and I hope to continue doing so for a while to come.

Thanks again,

xxx

More Books by Cyan Tayse

Pocket Rocket Novellas

(Steamy FF and FFM romance)
Have you Ever…?
Blank Canvas
A Gift to Remember

Brief Encounters Novellas

(Sweet MM romance)
Thick as Thieves
Secondhand Lover

Sweetwater Close

(Fairytale inspired stories)
The Suitor (*MM*)
The Moniker (*FF*)

Connect with the Author

http://www.cyantayse.weebly.com

https://www.facebook.com/CyanTayse

https://www.Twitter.com/cyan_tayse

https://www.instagram.com/cyantayse

https://www.amazon.com/author/cyantayse

https://www.bookbub.com/authors/cyan-tayse

About the Author

Cyan Tayse is the pen name of a multi-genre author based in New Zealand. After a lot of coaxing from friends, she decided to embark on a journey of discovery. Yes, that's right, she embraced her desire to write things a little different to her usual, thus the Pocket Rocket and Brief Encounters novellas were born.

Cyan can often be found lurking on social media, and she loves to hear from fellow authors and readers.

CPSIA information can be obtained
at www.ICGtesting.com
Printed in the USA
LVHW091721070922
727717LV00011B/267

9 780473 649869